MY CHRISTMAS ̲ ̲E

S J CRABB

♥

Copyrighted Material

CONTENTS

ALSO BY S J CRABB

More books by S J Crabb

The Diary of Madison Brown

My Perfect Life at Cornish Cottage

My Christmas Boyfriend

Jetsetters

More from Life

A Special Kind of Advent

Fooling in love

Will You

Holly Island

Aunt Daisy's Letter

The Wedding at the Castle of Dreams

sjcrabb.com

MY CHRISTMAS ROMANCE

Christmas comes once a year. True love comes once in a lifetime.

A heart-warming and uplifting story about finding love at Christmas.

Polly Proudlock was in a rut. Working at the cracker factory was beginning to lose its attraction and having just been dumped by her boyfriend, she had reached an all-time low.

The fact he was still her boss added to her problems, not to mention having to work alongside her replacement was a step too far.

A chance meeting changed everything, and Polly found herself agreeing to be a stranger's fake girlfriend for Christmas to their mutual benefit.

Miles Carlton was the perfect boyfriend. He took her to places she never thought she'd see, and Christmas soon took on a new meaning. Suddenly, she was seeing it through fresh eyes and she liked it—a lot.

As the snow falls and the magic of Christmas captures her heart, Polly discovers that she's no longer faking something that will only end in tears.

Then an opportunity presents itself that could change her life. But Christmas is fast approaching and she is running out of time.

Fate works in mysterious ways and their worlds are set on a collision course. Soon they are fighting for more than their own Happy Ever After and when the snow melts, who or what will be left standing?

CHAPTER 1

*W*hy do I always break the rules? I'm an idiot and always have been.

"What are you having?"

"A large Americano, please."

"Since when?"

"Since I decided to change it up a little, starting with my beverage choice."

"But you always drink tea."

"I always dated idiots too but I'm kind of hoping to break that habit as well."

Susie looks at me with the standard issue sympathy that I'm getting used to these days.

"Richie?"

"How did you guess?"

"What has he done?"

"Used and abused me and moved on to the next in line."

"He's an idiot, in fact, all men are idiots. There's a requirement by law that every young boy learns how to be an idiot by the time he leaves school, it's a fact."

1

She grins and I almost crack a smile, but I'm starting to think I've forgotten how.

"So, maybe it's time to move on, you know, fresh pastures and all that. Maybe we can sign you up for Dream Beginnings, I've only heard good things about that site."

"No!"

"Why not?"

"Because I'm not desperate."

"You are." She grins to take the sting from her words, but we both know she's right. I think I was born desperate and nothing I ever do works out.

Sighing, I shrug and smile bitterly.

"Not yet, let me wallow in self-pity for a little while. Besides, I haven't worked my way through the required ton of ice cream yet and watched movies on misery and revenge to set me on the right path."

"That's just procrastinating."

"So…"

"So, you need to show what's his face that you are over him already, moving on and never looking back."

"I wish it were that simple."

"It is."

"This time it's not because he's my boss, in case you've forgotten, and when I said he's moved on to the next in line, I wasn't joking. The 'next in line' stands beside me on the novelty line, Gail Donaldson, if you need to know the boyfriend thief's name for future reference."

"Bad luck."

"Luck has nothing to do with it. I always knew she liked him and well, he's such an idiot he was reeled in like a wet fish the moment she asked him for a 'private' word."

"Shameless."

"You're telling me. I was swept aside for a younger model who probably goes all the way on the first date."

"Sex is a powerful weapon, I should know."

She grins as she jumps up to fetch my order, and I feel the depression settle around me like an old friend.

Yes, we've been here before and I'm kind of bored with the company I keep. Depression needs to find a new friend because I am so done with it.

The rain pounds the pavement outside adding to my mood and I sigh as I stare at the steamed-up windows of the coffee shop. Fake Christmas trees, tinsel and festive tunes just reinforce the fact I'm alone again for Christmas. What a loser.

"Here you go, get that down you, it's not that bad."

Taking a sip of the coffee, I beg to differ and wrinkle my nose up in disgust. Horrible! Hot and strong, I prefer mine weak and sweet.

Susie looks thoughtful, which is not a good sign.

"We need a plan."

"No, thank you. I've been on the receiving end of one of your plans before and they never end well. No, I'll just have to learn to live with the fact I've been dumped by my boss before Christmas, leaving me to work alongside him and his new squeeze, reinforcing how sad my life is."

"Ok, I'll admit that was a bad plan, but I've got just the pick me up you need."

"Please no, I just want to retreat to my bed and pretend this isn't happening."

"You'd be doing me a favour."

"The answer's still no. I know what your favours end up costing me. The last time I did you a favour, they escorted me from the premises and I ended up walking home because I had no money for a cab and the trains weren't running. I got followed by a weirdo and ended up in the back of a police van when I reported him and they offered me a lift."

"I remember that, in fact, you were more than grateful

when you went out for dinner with the nice police officer who gave you a ride home."

"Exactly, that's just my point. He turned out to be engaged and just looking for a last fling before his wedding, so from now on I'm in charge of my own destiny. This time I'm going to hold out for the fairy-tale and only Prince Charming need apply."

"Good luck with that."

"Thank you."

Susie looks at her phone and gasps. "I'm so late, I should go."

"Late for what?"

"Kevin."

"What do you mean?"

"He's coming over, I said I'd be there."

"It's lunch time, doesn't he work like one hour from here?"

"He's out in the field, which means a nice cosy lunch with yours truly."

She winks and heads out like the whirlwind she is leaving me staring dejectedly at my hated coffee. I couldn't even get that right. I hate coffee and coffee hates me because when people ask for their regular coffee, I know just what they mean. Coffee always goes right through me, so with a groan, I push it away and contemplate another afternoon watching Richie and Gail flirt shamelessly over the novelty items production line.

CHAPTER 2

"Why am I still here, in fact, why did I even apply for this job in the first place? When I left school, I was going to be a famous model and actress; a rock star. The fact I did nothing about it isn't the point. I was desperate to leave home and prove I was capable of being an adult and this was the first job that actually replied to my application, surprising when my interests stated travelling and a weird obsession with James Bond.

I even contemplated moving near to Pinewood Studios in the vain hope I would be discovered as the next Bond girl. In fact, my success was guaranteed because if you want something badly enough you get it, right?

Wrong. I got the job on the production line in the cracker factory and I haven't moved on. Three years I've been here and made a grave error, I dated my boss.

Richie Banks, smooth talking criminal with slicked back hair and bedroom eyes. He charmed his way into mine and I thought we were the new power couple of the factory.

I was flattered by the attention. He was relentless in his pursuit of me and for a while I thought I had everything I ever wanted. A job, a nice home that I share with my crazy best friend and a boyfriend who was exciting and management. I enjoyed the looks of wonder in the other workers eyes as he sidled up to me and planted a kiss on my cheek, whispering dirty words in my ear and making me wish for 5 pm already. The fact it wasn't exactly professional didn't matter. He was the boss, the supervisor and so in our eyes, God.

The walk to the factory is becoming increasingly difficult because there is nothing inside for me anymore. Stuffing novelty items into crackers was never my life's ambition, and increasingly I'm discovering I want more. But what? I never excelled academically, and university was never an option. My parents divorced when I was five and mums had three new families since then. My dad joined the Navy and is always on manoeuvres, although he did manage to take a week off and marry a woman who lives in Thailand most of the time. In fact, we've never met which is a little suspicious but he seems happy, so that's fine by me.

Moving in with Susie Mahoney was the best thing I ever did because she is my sister from another mother. We share the same sense of humour, the same passions, and have the same taste in films and food. She is messy, I am neat and tidy. She is rubbish with money, I am the reincarnation of Scrooge. She doesn't care what people think of her and I care a little too much, so we complement each other perfectly, which is a very good thing as we appear to be stuck with each other because nobody else wants the job.

Thinking about Susie entertaining Kevin makes me laugh. They've been dating for a few months, but I've never met him. He always comes round when I'm at work because apparently, he works nights. They have a strange relationship, but at least they have one.

Maybe it's a good thing he works nights because so does

Susie. I was a little disturbed by her career choice, but she assured me it was all fine and just a bit of fun, a means to an end and money in the bank.

Susie works for an agency that specialises in supplying a date for men who need a partner to accompany them to functions. An escort, a companion and Susie assures me it's all above board. She gets to go to some fabulous places and is paid to do so. The men she meets are interesting and perfect gentlemen, and she gets paid well for enjoying a night out every so often. She tried to get me involved once, but it ended up with me being thrown out on the streets because the man's wife tracked him down. He ushered me out of the side door with no coat or cab fare, leaving me to walk the streets of Harpenden alone and afraid. It ended up with another nightmare when Roger the police officer rescued me. Some rescuer he turned out to be, leaving me thinking that every man out there is a predator of the worst kind.

As I approach the staff entrance, I shiver inside. Lunch time is over and I need to endure three more hours of monotony before I can race home and snuggle up on the settee with a bag of popcorn and the thriller series that I'm halfway through.

I can see Gail in the distance looking pretty and wholesome in her cream Puffa jacket with fur around the collar. She looks like Baby Spice, all sweet and innocent with a soft edge and dewy eyes. Her pearly white teeth flash in a smile as she nods to Harry, the security man who sits hunched over his newspaper while the workers file past him back to monotony.

I join the line and don't even get a raised eye in my direction as I punch in and head to my locker.

Gail is stowing away a jacket that makes mine look dreary and dowdy and I hear her high voice say with excitement, "Richie's taking me ice skating tonight. I can't wait, he's so romantic. You know, he even cut my toast into a heart shape this morning when he brought it to me in bed."

Toast in bed, I would hate that. Think of the crumbs. He never made me toast in bed. In fact, it was always me making him a fry up at 6 am most days. I was such a mug. I thought that's what a good girlfriend did. Look after her man and the way to keep the flame burning was through his appetite, both physical and sexual.

I was a fool because girls like Gail have it all worked out. If I didn't hate her so much, I would be impressed. Picturing Richie serving up heart shaped toast in those disgusting Y fronts he insisted made him look sexy, makes me smile inside. Lucky escape comes to mind as I contemplate my future without him in it.

By the time I've reached my position on the production line, I'm feeling a little better. Who needs Richie Banks, not me? I'm a Bond girl and should start acting like one. This time next year I will be spending Christmas in Monte Carlo, or the Seychelles. It's time to put the past behind me and seize the future I always wanted, and as soon as Christmas is over, I am going to do something about it.

"Polly!"

I look up as Richie stands glaring at me with a stern expression, looking at the watch on his wrist and tapping his foot. "You're late."

"Not really."

I stare in disbelief at the clock that has just moved past the hour and he rolls his eyes. "Timekeeping is key, especially when we work to deadlines. It may only be a minute to you but add it to the other minutes you let pass throughout the days, the weeks, the months and we have a serious problem."

"But…"

"No buts, Polly, just shape up and make sure you're a

minute later leaving. I won't tell you again. Next time you will receive a written warning."

He turns and I notice that Gail has slipped into her place and is working away as if she was there before, even though she was later than me. Marion, the lady to my right, throws me a sympathetic look and shakes her head as Richie whispers something in Gail's ear to make her giggle. I can just imagine the dirty words he used, and feel the sting of tears threatening to reveal my misery.

"Don't let him see you cry." Marion whispers above the sound of the machinery and I nod gratefully. Wise words from a wise woman. Marion has worked here for twenty years and has seen it all. God forbid I follow in her footsteps. I need to get out, but how and where do I go?

CHAPTER 3

*A*t precisely one minute past five, I leave my post and head to my locker feeling as if I'm carrying the weight of the world on my shoulders. Gail is changing into her white furry snow boots and gorgeous jacket and I watch as she shakes her hair out from the ponytail she wears for work and her golden hair spills down her back like a sheet of pure gold. I try not to look, but Richie sidles up behind her and spins her around to face him and lowers his lips to hers in a passionate kiss.

"Get a room already."

Somebody shouts from further in the room and the laughter echoes around us as we all watch a public show of affection that is in the worst possible taste.

"Disgusting."

Marion leans in and whispers, "That man has no shame, her either."

"It's fine."

"Keep telling yourself that, darlin', he's not worth it. Men like that never are. Mark my words, he'll be after the next bit of skirt who bats her eyelashes at him before the summer. I've seen it all before, men, they're disgusting."

"Not all men, Marion."

Cindy, a sweet girl who just joined us six months ago, smiles prettily. "My Darren is the exception. He wouldn't behave like that; I just know it."

We share a smile and Marion nods. "He *is* the exception."

Cindy looks so happy it restores my faith a little. Darren Benstock is one of the warehouse packers and they have been dating for one month. He is kind, sweet and loving and thinks the world of Cindy. They share their breaks and he is always looking for excuses to seek her out during the day and if anything, I want to find a man like Darren. Steady, dependable, and loyal. Who doesn't want that?

Gail's giggle is seriously grating on my nerves, and then she squeals when Richie dips her to the floor and kisses her relentlessly. Marion puts her hand on my arm and says sympathetically, "It will get better. Just rise above it and count yourself lucky you're off the hook. There's someone way better for you out there my girl, just give it time."

"Thanks, Marion."

We walk out together and she shivers. "I can't stand this weather; it freezes me to the bone. The bus was late yesterday and I thought I'd die from hypothermia."

"The trains aren't much better."

"Typical public transport, there must be something better than that."

"Bicycles perhaps?"

We share a laugh because the thought of either of us wobbling through the traffic on two wheels is something nobody should ever have to see.

"That's better."

"What?"

"Seeing you laugh. You're a pretty girl and Richie's a fool."

11

"Maybe. You know, Marion, I think I'm giving men up for a while. I'm better on my own, I know where I am then."

Marion rolls her eyes. "I give you a week. Get yourself out there, girl, and show Richie what he's missing. You're young and there's plenty more where he came from but don't settle for anything less than you deserve."

"Thanks, I'll bear that in mind."

We part company and I begin the slow walk to the station thinking about my life. A lone flake of snow lands on my lip and I lick it away. It's quickly followed by another until there is soon quite a flurry. Shivering, I pull my coat a little tighter. There must be more to life than this, surely.

～

Susie is waiting, looking absolutely wrecked and I raise my eyes. "Hard day?"

"Kevin came."

"Spare me the details."

We giggle and she fans herself with her hand. "Who needs central heating?"

"I do. Oh, and an open fire wouldn't go amiss either. Perhaps an electric blanket too, that may do the trick."

"I can think of better ways to get warm."

"I'm not interested in your ways."

Heading to the kitchen, I only have one thing on my mind. A mug of builder's tea and the packet of digestives I know should be waiting.

Susie follows me in and jumps up on the worktop, her legs swinging against the cupboards. "Polly…"

"No."

"You don't know what I'm going to say."

"Whatever it is, the answer is no."

"Don't be like that, I wouldn't ask but…"

"But what?"

"Well, it's just that I've kind of double booked myself and in the spirit of generosity, I thought you could use the money."

"What money?"

"The money you would earn for just a couple of hours of your time."

"No."

"You don't even know what it is yet."

"I can hazard a guess, and the only thing I want to do is curl up on the settee in my pyjamas with Netflix to keep me company."

Susie groans. "But it's so easy. All you have to do is go to a stupid party and mingle. The money is good."

"No."

I head to my room and close the door on her. The thought of going out again in this hostile cold environment is not an attractive prospect. Neither is mingling with strangers, no matter how much she will pay me.

I only have one leg in my fleecy elephant pyjama bottoms before she bursts in and throws herself on the bed and my mercy. "It's just that…"

"What?" I stare at her in exasperation and she blushes. "I kind of need the flat this evening."

"For what?"

I stare at her in surprise and she looks a little shady. "Um, Kevin wants to come around for dinner. I'm cooking and everything."

"You cooking, that I don't believe. You've got Uber eats on speed dial and don't even know where the saucepans live."

"Pleeeease Polly, pretty please. As I said, the money's good and it will make you forget about Richie for a few hours."

"But I don't want to."

She looks shocked and I say hastily, "Go out, I mean. I do

want to forget about Richie, but the thriller I'm watching promises a psycho murderer and I'm kind of looking forward to picturing Richie as the victim. So, as you can see, I have plans."

"Two hours, that's all it's for. I'll be your best friend."

She smiles at me like an eager puppy and I sigh wearily. "How much money?"

"Two hundred."

"What!"

"I told you the money was good."

"What's the job? I don't have to do anything, um, unsavoury do I?"

"Of course not, he just wants a date to a party, end of."

"Where is it?"

She looks excited and tucks her legs under her as she perches on a bed that I would much rather be spending time in than gallivanting across town meeting a mystery man. "That's the best part, it's at the Luton Hoo." Her excitement is almost rubbing off on me, but then I remember something important.

"But I have nothing to wear, that place is well out of my league."

"That's the beauty of it, I already have your outfit. It arrived when you were at work."

She jumps up and rushes from the room before returning almost immediately with a brightly coloured box tied with ribbon.

"The agency sent this over. It's your costume."

"What costume, what is this party?"

"Fancy dress." She claps her hands and looks excited. "You see, it's perfect for you. All you have to do is wear this, meet your partner and spend two hours tops with him pretending you're on a date. Then the agency will pay me two hundred pounds, which of course I will give straight to you. Perfect."

She laughs happily and I have to admit it does sound easy. "How will I get there?"

"Cab. There's one booked for seven, so you have time to glam up and grab a bite to eat. What do you fancy?"

She seizes her phone and I wince. "Forget Uber eats, I've got a pasta dish with my name on it in the fridge."

"So, you'll do it?"

"Do I have a choice?"

"Not really." She grins and her expression reflects how grateful she is. Goodness, she must really like Kevin to pass up the opportunity to earn £200 and party with the privileged. I can't wait to meet him.

CHAPTER 4

"*I* can't wear this."

The horror on the face that is staring out at me from the mirror reflects how I feel inside. Susie laughs gaily. "You look amazing, it suits you."

"Are you serious? I look like an idiot. It's indecent."

"Hardly."

"Is this guy for real, did he seriously choose this outfit?"

"He was very specific. What does it matter, you only have to wear it for two hours in public and nobody will know it's you anyway?"

"I'll know."

"Oh, come on, Polly, where's your spirit of adventure, reckless abandonment and sense of fun? This promises to be an amazing experience."

"For who? It's like a sick form of torture to me."

She stands beside me and it strikes me how pretty she looks tonight. She has made a huge effort and her newly washed hair gleams and her make-up is sultry and provocative. The red dress that clings to her body looks designer and she's even wearing killer heels – at home. She must really like Kevin which is the only reason I sigh and say wearily, "Two hours tops."

"I knew you wouldn't let me down."

"I've let myself down though, thank God no one will know it's me."

She hands me an envelope and a shoulder bag, that will be swallowed up inside my costume, containing money and a phone.

"Have fun, babe, I can't wait to hear all about it."

"Same."

We share a smile and despite everything I hope she has fun tonight. I only want the best for my dearest friend which is why I'm agreeing to this farce in the first place.

I can tell she wants to laugh and I roll my eyes. "Don't say it, I'm only doing this because you begged me to. If the guy's seriously odd, I'm slipping out the side door and calling a cab, just saying."

Snapping my mask in place, I stare at the ridiculous image staring back at me. Total weirdo. What man in his right mind chooses to go to Luton Hoo, the home of luxury, dressed as Batman and Robin. An obvious nutcase, that's who.

THE CAB DRIVER can't keep a straight face as he relays every superhero joke in his repartee and by the time we reach our destination, I have heard it all. Luckily, the cab was prepaid, so I just give him a tip and head towards the most amazing building I never get to see first hand.

Luton Hoo is an exclusive hotel and only the wealthy ever get to experience its delights. Tonight's party is some kind of industry one and the man I'm meeting is a businessman here for the event and obviously in need of a date. I still can't get my head around the fact that Susie loves this kind of thing. She has gone all over the place on the arms of many men and is showered in designer outfits and gifts that make me a little jealous. Strictly above board though and no funny business allowed and sometimes I almost give in to her demands that I give this occupation a try. I mean, being an escort isn't shady, not really. Its only what other people think, anyway, but Susie's not like that. She's just gregarious and fun and wants to live a little. I only hope Kevin is understanding of it because any normal guy would hate the thought of his girl-friend earning her living as the companion of a rich business man, no matter how innocent it all is.

As I walk inside, I hand the invitation to the man standing proudly at the door and he nods. "Ma'am."

I'm glad of my mask because I'm sure I must be looking pretty embarrassed right now and almost don't appreciate the amazing décor of a place decked out in Christmas grotto finery. It's like seeing the North Pole in a millionaire's mansion. Grand, beautiful and dripping in opulence, with the sound of an impressive piano guiding me through the array of fine costumes and wealthy attendees.

It feels a little surreal as I take a glass from a passing waiter and sip the champagne for a little Dutch courage. All I need to do is find my Batman and then this show can get on the road.

All around me are amazing costumes and I wish he had chosen better. The lycra is seriously revealing and my body was not meant to be forced into something that shows every lump and bump, not to mention my insanely out of control upper half. The black boots I'm wearing, reach my knees and the tights rub against my thighs as I walk through Cinderel-las, Prince Charmings, pirates and cowboys. No Batman though and I feel as if I'm missing my right arm.

The music is seductive and the temperature in the room

warm and cosy. It feels good being here and ordinarily I would be super excited to be here at all. But I feel nervous and apprehensive, which doesn't get any better when a soft voice whispers behind me, "You made it."

Spinning around, I stare up at two glittering blue eyes hidden behind the black mask and see a man staring at me who definitely *does* suit his costume. He is just my type on paper, tall, muscular and strong and I watch in awe at the cape swirling around his shoulders, making me feel a little breathless. He winks and holds out his hand. "Bruce Wayne, but you can call me Batman."

"Pussy Galore, but you can call me Robin."

Am I insane? Did I really just say my name was Pussy Galore? His eyes sparkle with laughter and I giggle self-consciously, "Sorry, that came out wrong, I'm a bit of a Bond freak and it was the first name that came to mind."

He leans in and whispers, "So, Pussy, I'm guessing you'd like a Martini, shaken, not stirred."

"Sounds good."

He winks and takes my arm, leading me towards the bar which gives me a moment to gather my senses. Wow, Batman is hot, super hot. No old weirdo for me tonight. This man is not only a super hero, he's all my fantasies rolled into one intoxicating package. Why on earth does he need to pay for a date?

CHAPTER 5

*I*t feels a little surreal being here. Usually I would be tucked up in bed by now, trying not to think of Richie and how he humiliated me. Fate is a strange one because instead I'm walking beside a man I have no business being with. He's confident, in control and rather intriguing, and it all feels like a dream. There's a nagging voice in my head that won't go away, telling me I'm only here because he paid me to and it's not one I want to hear because I'm not sure I like how that makes me feel.

"Take this and relax."

He grabs another fluted glass from a passing waiter and hands it to me before taking one for himself.

"How do you know I'm not relaxed?" I say defensively and he smiles. "Because I can tell. You're stiff and nervous and keep on looking around you as if you expect something bad to happen. Just relax and enjoy the experience."

"Do you blame me for feeling a little nervous, I mean, it's not every day I dress up like a superhero and meet a total stranger."

"Isn't it?"

"No."

I feel uncomfortable as I realise how pathetic that sounded. Of course, he thinks this is my job and I do this all the time and why would he think any differently?

Again, I'm not sure how I feel about that. This may be fun and interesting for people like Susie who don't care what people think of them, but it matters to me.

Suddenly, I feel like a fraud and turn to him and say anxiously, "Listen, I'm sorry but I have to go."

"Where?" He looks confused and I feel bad.

"Home, actually. This was a mistake."

I can feel myself blushing as I stare at him awkwardly and see his eyes flash a little as he looks at me with irritation.

Then, to my surprise, he takes the drink from my hand and sets it down on a nearby table and grabs my hand firmly, dragging me after him. It makes me panic a little as I realise I may have got myself into a situation I may not be able to control and am surprised when he leads me onto the dance floor and takes me in his arms.

"What are you doing?" I hiss, feeling a little out of sorts as his hands wrap around my waist and he pulls me close.

Leaning down, he murmurs, "Just relax and don't over-think this. Firstly, from the moment I met you, I could tell you were nervous. Secondly, Pussy Galore wouldn't run from danger, she would embrace it and seize the moment and thirdly, where would Batman be without Robin? Like I said, just relax and enjoy your evening. I'm an ok kind of guy who only wants company for this infernal gathering with no strings and no consequences."

"Why?" Now it's my turn to ask him a question.

"Why, what?"

"Why do you need pay for a date? I'm sure you must have a little black book, isn't that what most men consult when they need a date? Why pay for a stranger?"

"Because it's easier, no fuss and no awkward parting of the ways when it's over. No expectations and no need to pretend this is anything more than it is."

"That sounds pretty sad to me."

"That's because you overthink things."

"How do you know I overthink things? Any normal person would think it weird."

He pulls back a little and looks at me with a quizzical expression, and the light in his eyes dances as he smirks. "From where I'm dancing, you don't get to call me out on being weird. You're the one dressed as Robin going under the name Pussy Galore. You agreed to be my date for money, which makes you..."

"That's it, I'm leaving."

I pull away angrily and start moving quickly to the door. How dare he insinuate I'm some kind of desperate woman who sells herself to the highest bidder? He has made me out to be cheap and at this moment in time, that's exactly how I feel.

Before I reach the door, a hand grabs mine and pulls me back and spins me around against a broad chest. Strong arms wrap around me and close the whole world out. Even the music blends into the background as a husky voice whispers, "I'm sorry. Please don't leave."

For a moment, I relax against his chest and hear his heart beating, which shows me that at least he has one. It feels good being locked in his arms and if anything, I feel a little foolish as I sigh. "Ok, two hours, will that be long enough?"

He doesn't let me go and his breath blows hot against my ear as he says softly, "Possibly."

"What do you mean, possibly? It will have to be because that was the arrangement."

"What if I want a different arrangement?"

The warning bells are threatening to deafen me, and I tense in shock. I'm going to kill Susie, I knew it.

I make to pull away and his soft laughter appears to mock my indignation as he breathes, "Relax, it's nothing sinister. Hear me out and then maybe we can start again."

To be honest, I feel a little intrigued because this is an odd situation, so I nod and he pulls away and steers me to the side of the room, towards two chairs set around a table in an alcove. Despite the party going on all around us, it feels a little intimate and my own heart starts racing as I wonder what he is going to ask.

I feel nervous when he fixes me with a look that is most definitely now business and leans in, saying firmly, "I have a business proposition for you."

Here it comes.

Preparing myself mentally for what I suspect is coming, I stare at him with a hard expression.

He seems almost nervous and that alone surprises me because from the moment I met him, he has appeared anything but. However, there's a sadness in his eyes that makes me wonder who, or what put it there, and he has a lost look about him that I completely understand.

He appears to be wrestling with something and searching for words, and then he says slowly, "Listen. I'm only in town for a few weeks over Christmas and am looking for a companion to be my plus one because I need to keep my head in business with none of the distractions that dating brings. I want a professional. Somebody used to dealing with these kinds of situations and not someone who will expect a marriage proposal at the end. One hundred percent a business arrangement and at the end of it we part company and carry on with our lives. So, Pussy Galore, are you up for that, I'll pay you well, it is a business deal after all?"

I can't believe what I'm hearing. Now I know how Julia

Roberts felt in Pretty Woman. This man appears much the same as Richard Gere, cold, businesslike and cool and paying for something most people have to work hard to enjoy. Then again, it's an attractive proposition. I'm not looking for any emotional attachment either. I'm alone at Christmas, as usual, and have nothing in my diary except for work and Netflix. Can I do this; should I do this? He is looking at me with interest as if I'm just another deal he's negotiating and I feel a little powerful if I'm honest. He wants *me*, well, Susie actually, but he doesn't know I'm not her. He thinks I do this all the time. Maybe I should, it's certainly more interesting than stuffing crackers and at least it would get me out of an evening.

I'm not sure what changes from my earlier outrage, but I find myself nodding slowly and saying in a stilted voice. "Ok, until Christmas then."

"No, Pussy."

"Um, do you mind not calling me that, it was a bad choice of name and feels a little award if I'm honest."

"What is your name then?"

A thousand reasons why I should keep an air of mystery clamour to be heard and I find myself blurting out, "Susie Mahoney."

"So, Susie Mahoney, will you be my Christmas girlfriend?"

"No strings, just a dating companion. No funny business."

"No funny business."

His eyes twinkle and I hold my breath as I jump feet first into the unknown.

"Why, *no,* though? I thought you said until Christmas."

"I said over Christmas. Past New Year and then the deal breaks."

"I'm sorry Batman, or can I call you Bruce, what are you asking me exactly?"

He leans forward, takes my hands and says softly, "I need you to be my girlfriend and not just at evening events. I want you to come home with me for Christmas and be my girlfriend. My family need to think we're an item because it's the only way I can convince them that I'm doing ok."

There is something he's not telling me because why does it matter if he's alone or not, but then again, who I am to argue with his reasons?

The fact he's holding my hands is a little odd. Nice but odd but he seems genuine and just a little bit gorgeous, so I shrug and say in a business like voice. "We will take this one date at a time. If I'm comfortable with it, I'll go all the way – I mean, to the New Year, I don't mean well, you know what I mean, it's just that…"

His finger silences my words and he laughs softly. "I know what you mean and that was never an option. You're safe with me because this is purely a business arrangement as friends. All I need is for you to go along with what I say and make my family believe we're together. Will you accept the job, please?"

"Ok, on one condition."

He nods and offers me a small smile, "Name it."

"The money goes to charity."

"Why?"

"Because I need you to know before we start, something I may not be able to reason with myself. I'm only here to help out a friend. I don't do this normally and I'm not comfortable being paid money for my, um, services. I'll do it because I have nothing better to do and then, if I'm uncomfortable, or discover I can't stand the sight of you, I can walk away with no hard feelings with my dignity intact."

For a moment, he stares at me in confusion and then says slowly, "You did what?"

I squirm a little as I face up to the fact he may be angry

that I'm not the professional he paid for. Then he shakes his head and looks at me a little differently, "You did this to help a friend, are you mad?"

"Not mad, just easily manipulated."

He laughs and I can't help but join him. Now I've said it, I do feel a little foolish and he smiles and says with a hint of respect, "Then you are the perfect woman for the job. Will you take it, the job I mean, for charity, of course."

"Of course." We share a smile and I make my mind up in an instant. What the hell, this could be the most fun I've had in years.

CHAPTER 6

"So, what happens now?"

"We have some fun."

"I don't mean that, shouldn't we get our story straight because if we're supposed to be dating, wouldn't it appear a bit odd if we know nothing about one another?"

"Good point, you go first."

"No, you."

He rolls his eyes and holds out his hand, gripping mine in an iron grip and shaking it hard.

"Hi, my name is Miles Carlton. I'm 29 years old and approaching 30 with horror. I live alone in London, which suits me just fine, and I work in mergers and acquisitions for Henry Lloyd Ltd. I like polo, travelling and skiing. I went to university at St Andrew's, the same one as Kate and William, and that's my only claim to fame. My family live locally and I have one sister and a brother who I rarely see. I'm single by choice because the last woman I dated cheated on me with my brother and then ran off with his best friend."

"Oh."

I'm a little speechless because that's horrible. Instinctively, I reach out and grasp his hand as he says tightly, "I don't want your sympathy. I'm over it."

"But your brother…"

"Is fine. We moved on. I won't let a woman come between us, we're better than that. Anyway, it's your turn now."

I should come clean, I should tell him but to be honest I'm still putting up walls to hide behind, so I say carefully, "Ok, my name is Susie Mahoney and I'm what's considered a good friend, well, I like to think so, anyway. I live locally in a rented flat and have a job in um, production, which pays the bills with not a lot left over. I'm 21 and have worked the same job since I left school after a less than impressive grade average. My family are scattered and I don't mean their ashes, as they are very much alive and living their lives without needing me in it. My mum lives in Preston with her new husband and their kids, two of which are hers from husband number two and two of them his from wife number one. I visit when required, which suits me just fine."

"And your father?"

I hate the sympathy in his eyes and say defensively, "He works away. He's in the navy and is at sea - a lot. He's also married to a woman I've never met and weirdly I think he's only met her twice."

"You're kidding."

"I wish I was. She lives in Thailand, which is strange because she hasn't been here once that I know of."

I see the distaste on his face and swallow the lump in my throat. I know my family is rubbish, a waste of space that never should have had children. It appears that my life is poles apart from his privileged one which makes me feel embarrassed and as if I'm not worthy and I don't like how I feel right now.

As I look down, he lifts my face to his and the look in his eyes takes my breath away.

"Your parents must be very proud of you, Susie Mahoney, you're a credit to them."

A lump forms in my throat as I look into those blue eyes who are not judging me on my unconventional beginnings. Instead, he gives me the courage to blurt out, "I lied."

He drops his hand and looks disappointed.

"I see."

"I'm not Susie Mahoney, my name's Polly. I should have told you, but I was scared in case you were a weirdo."

"Maybe I am."

I smile gently. "No, you're not. Maybe a little confused though, I mean, who chooses to dress as Batman in their spare time when they could have been Prince Charming?"

He looks away and I see a tight expression cross his face as he says tersely, "I'm no Prince Charming, Polly, you would do well to remember that."

My heart sinks, of course, this no fairy tale, just business.

He snaps out of it and sighs. "Well, we should get this show on the road. If we see anyone we know, this is how things are. We met online, say six months ago and as luck would have it, you live near my parents. It's early days but we're enjoying getting to know one another and taking things slowly."

"That sounds like a plan." I nod my approval and then we hear, "Miles."

A deep voice interrupts our business meeting, and I watch Miles wince a little as he stands and shakes the man's hand.

"Simon, it's good to see you, but how did you know it was me?"

"Your father told me you'd be here and mentioned you were coming as Batman, but what I want to know is, who on earth this delightful Robin is?"

His attention turns to me and I squirm a little.

"Meet Polly, my girlfriend."

The man looks a little shocked, and I detect a faint look of triumph on Miles' face as he stares at the man dressed as a cowboy.

"I'm pleased to meet you, my dear. I don't think I've seen you around before and I know all the lovely ladies around here."

"I don't get out much, you know, work always gets in the way." I smile politely, although inside I'm a mass of nerves.

"What do you do?"

"I'm in production, anyway, I'm so sorry, but if you'll excuse me, I really need to use the um, restroom. I'm sorry to be rude."

The men nod and I make a quick getaway before any more awkward questions get thrown my way. As I walk to find the ladies' room, I curse my luck. How will this work? The first hurdle almost made me stumble, and by the look in Miles' eyes, he wasn't happy about speaking to that man. I wonder who he was? He looked to be in his fifties. Are they related, connected by business?

Once again, cursing him for his costume choice, I shrug out of the whole clinging mess, just to do what comes naturally and wonder if this was such a good idea. Miles seems nice, so it seems out of character to want to deceive his family, and why am I allowing myself to help him?

I can't even call Susie for advice because no doubt she's hard at it with Kevin. I'm not sure what to do and just sit for a moment in my cubicle and worry about this strange position I've got myself into.

Then I think of Richie and Gail, probably ice skating under a romantic moon as we speak. We never did things like that. The most romantic thing we ever did was go bowling one night and have sex in his car on the way home. My life sucks and even now it's not much better. Miles is a man every girl dreams of finding. Rich, successful, gorgeous and educated. He's already good company, and I've only known him for less than an hour. At least I would have some fun for a change, and maybe I should just accept this for what it is. An adventure and a moment in time when Polly Proudlock did something extraordinary. I suppose what makes up my mind is picturing the look on the faces of my colleagues when I boast about my new boyfriend and the places we will go.

Gail will be green with envy and Richie will have his face rubbed into the fact I'm over him already. The fog of indecision clears and I see it all as clear as the sun in a bright cloudless sky. I will use Miles as he is using me. To make me look good and keep everyone from knowing the real story. Yes, this arrangement may just work well for both of us.

CHAPTER 7

*a*s I make my way back to Miles, I pass many amazing outfits, princesses with their princes, storybook characters, elves and fairies, all looking amazing in their finery. Me, on the other hand, I look ridiculous and yet the anonymity of the mask makes me braver in their company than I would normally feel.

In fact, I am feeling quite good about myself at the moment because I have a feeling that anything's possible. This morning I would never have believed that I would be here now and Miles, despite the mask, is every fantasy I've ever had come to life.

I'm quite excited to see where this adventure will take me and as I see the man himself looking a little awkward as he talks to Simon, I smile.

He looks up with relief when he sees me and holds out his hand.

"If you'll excuse me, Simon, I really should hit the dance floor."

Simon nods and I feel a little uncomfortable as he looks

me up and down, his gaze lingering a little too long on my breasts.

Damn this lycra and its ability to highlight every imperfection I own.

Miles takes me into his arms and whispers, "I was just about to come and find you, that man's intolerable."

"Who is he?"

"Do you remember the girl I told you about?"

"What, the cheating ex?"

"Yes, that was her father."

"I'm sorry."

"It's fine, in fact more than fine because now he'll report back that I've moved on and may I say, with a considerably better model."

"How much have you had to drink?"

I smirk but love the compliment. Whoever this girl was must have been a hag because if he thinks I'm a better model, he *has* had too much to drink.

The music plays 'Last Christmas' by Wham and I love the fact I'm in a gorgeous man's arms, swaying to the music surrounded by the warm atmosphere of decadence. It certainly beats the evening I had planned, and I feel as if I could achieve anything in life. Miles seems happy to just sway along to the music and as evenings go, this one is shaping up to be one of the best.

I'm not sure how many songs we dance to, but when the tempo changes, he pulls back and grins.

"What do you say, shall we grab that Martini now, Ms Galore?"

"Oh Mr Bond, you smooth talker, if I didn't know better, I'd say you had an ulterior motive."

"Call me James and maybe I do."

He winks and I follow him off the dance floor towards

the bar area. After fighting our way through the crowd, we finally secure our drinks and look around with interest.

"Tell me again why you're here. I'm guessing you could have stayed home because apart from Simon, you haven't spoken to anyone else." I take a sip of my drink and wait for his answer with interest.

"You could be right, but then again, I wouldn't have met you."

"Or you could have saved yourself some money. I still don't really understand all this. Why do you need to prove to your family that you've moved on?"

His smile fades, making me regret my words, and he sighs. "Because ever since it happened, they have been treading on eggshells around me. Freddie, my brother, can't appear to look at me without a guilty expression and my parents keep on mentioning single girls to try and palm me off. I know they won't rest until I've met someone else, but quite frankly, I'm just not interested."

"I wouldn't mind a line of eligible men queueing outside my door, you *are* weird."

"Curses, my cover has been blown."

He winks and takes a sip of his drink and says thought-fully. "I thought there would have been men queueing at your door."

"I wish. No, the only man that ever did is now happily in lust with a Barbie doll. To make matters worse he's my boss and she works alongside me. I have to endure their endless flirting and snatched make out sessions in front of me and all I get are looks of sympathy from my coworkers who watched the whole sorry saga unfold. To add to my misery, my flatmate and best friend who should have been your date tonight, is so loved up it's making me feel even worse. I think I'm the only woman in the world alone this Christmas, which does little for my self-confidence."

"What about your mum, won't she expect you to go to her this Christmas, will she be upset?"

"Absolutely not. I'm sorry, Miles, don't get me wrong, I do love my mum but it's always been hard trying to fit in with her new families. I've always felt like a stranger, the odd one out, the visitor you know you must invite but dread coming. Mum does her best, but I know she feels guilty. I see it in her eyes, so I kind of understand what you mean when you say you're dreading seeing it in your own parents' ones. It's hard being an adult, isn't it? Hard to get things right and hard to find your place in life."

"Well, my little Bond girl, not this year. This year, it all changes because we've found one another. Two partners in crime who want the same thing - to get through the season and have some fun along the way. So, here's to having a good time this Christmas and making it one we will both never forget."

As THE EVENING GOES ON, I discover how much I'm enjoying his company. He's good fun, attentive and an attractive addition to my arm. He meets several acquaintances and we act like a couple and say the right things at the right time and by the end of the evening, have our lines off pat.

At eleven on the dot, Miles says gratefully, "Thanks Polly, I've had a great time, I hope you weren't too bored."

"No, on the contrary, I've had fun. Thanks for making it so easy for me."

It feels a little awkward as we stand at the point of departure and drawing my coat a little tighter around me, I smile. "Well, thank you. I mean it, I had a good time. Anyway, I think that's my cab, or at least I hope it is because it's got my name on it."

He laughs as he sees the man standing nearby, holding a card up with Susie Mahoney written in marker pen, just like they do at the airport.

"Then until the next time, Pussy Galore, I'm looking forward to it already."

He presses a card into my hand and says slightly nervously. "Regarding our arrangement, is it still on, I mean, are you ok with it?"

"I think so." I stare at him, feeling a little shy all of a sudden and he appears to relax a little.

"Give me your number and I'll be in touch. If you have a change of heart, no problem. It's just a nice thought to spend some more time with someone who is so natural and easy to be around."

I think I hold my breath as he whips out his phone from somewhere under his costume and hands it to me, watching as I punch in the details he needs should he decide to act on his offer. Part of me hopes he will, and the other part of me thinks I'm a fool if I think it will ever happen.

I shiver a little as the icy chill of winter reminds me that there's a reason why thin lycra costumes should be banned, not only in winter but full stop and I smile awkwardly. "Well, Mr Bond masquerading as Batman, I'll bid you goodnight. Until we meet again."

I don't wait for a response because I am now seriously freezing and just run towards my Uber like an Olympic sprinter.

As I settle down in the back of the warm and cosy taxi, I smile to myself. What a night! Now I know why Susie raves about it most of the time. Just for a moment back there I was somebody of importance. Not Polly Proudlock, stuffer of crackers and invisible girl. Tonight, I was a Bond girl dressed as a caped crusader and my partner in crime, my leading man, was the stuff of my dreams.

CHAPTER 8

I feel so frustrated and it's not just because I'm standing next to Gail, being forced to listen to her gushing over her *incredible* night with Richie. It's because Susie was fast asleep when I got home and never surfaced this morning. The flat was a complete mess and she must have thought better of cooking because Chinese takeaway cartons were all over the place. It was hard to ignore the mess because that sort of thing gives me palpitations, but I was exhausted despite the natural high that spending the evening with a hot guy gives you. I just stripped off the hated costume and crawled into my fleecy pyjamas, grateful that I was able to snuggle down in bed as I heard the rain lashing against the window. I think I fell asleep with a smile on my face that hasn't been there for some time.

"It was amazing, Richie was so strong and attentive as he held my hand, guiding me through the other skaters. I couldn't love him any more if I tried."

Marion nudges me as Cindy says kindly, "It sounds amazing."

She catches my eye and smiles nervously, almost as if she

feels guilty for commenting at all, and I smile reassuringly because Cindy is the type of girl who is too nice for her own good.

"I wish they would change things up around here."

Marion groans as she stuffs another cheap bottle opener into what's considered a luxury cracker.

"What do you mean, Marion?"

Gail lisps her question and I try to ignore the vision of me stuffing her head into the next cracker and let me tell you, it wouldn't be the luxury variety either. No, Gail deserves the value brand because she is that cheap. As I smirk at the image, Marion sighs beside me. "This stuff is so old. I've been here twenty years and I don't think they've ever changed the recipe. The same outdated items that nobody wants that end up in the bin and stale jokes and cheap paper hats. Where's the fun in it? Everyone knows what's inside and the element of surprise has gone, much like being married really."

"What do you mean?" Cindy's eyes are wide and Marion shrugs. "It all looks exciting on the outside but when you pull it, you realise the contents aren't worth the effort."

I laugh out loud and Gail says pityingly, "Goodness Marion, you really need a date night as a matter of urgency. Take Richie and me, I mean, he is always surprising me with little displays of affection. Do you know, he even gave me his mint from the restaurant we ate in last night, you know, the lovely gold luxurious one that comes with the bill. He's so romantic."

"Actually, he hates dark chocolate. He just didn't want it." I grin as Marion laughs out loud and Cindy hides her smile as Gail says with a slight edge to her voice, "Jealousy is not an attractive quality, Polly, you have let yourself down."

The silence surrounds me as my co workers wait for my reaction. To be honest, I think I've been pretty restrained about the whole thing until now. I've endured the constant digs and sniping, the gloating and the self-satisfied anecdotes of someone rubbing my nose firmly in my own misery, but this is a step too far. I feel the rage bubbling up inside and turn to hit her with the full force of my anger when Cindy whispers, "Who is that?"

The moment is interrupted and we all look up at the mezzanine level to see a smart woman dressed in a tailored suit with her hair looking as if she's fresh from the stylists. She's wearing high stilettos and her make-up looks carefully applied and professional and she is talking to Arthur, the owner of Sparkle Crackers, while he points out various things from their elevated level.

As I look at her, I feel even more worthless than I did before. This woman is chic perfection and the total opposite of a girl who is currently wearing a hair net and a pair of safety goggles while dressed in an overall. Where is such glamour in my life because she is glamorous, from her lacquered hair to her scuff free heels?

Marion lowers her voice. "I think she's the new hotshot marketing expert I heard Richie telling Jayden Price about the other day."

At the mention of her boyfriend, Gail says quickly, "You must mean Miss Constable. Oh, yes, he mentioned her to me a couple of days ago, you know, pillow talk and all that."

I pointedly turn my back on her and say with interest, "That's new."

"Not before time, if you ask me."

"What do you mean, Marion?"

"Well, sales aren't what they used to be and I don't know about you, but I've noticed a drop in production levels. They are working with half the workforce they used to have and I've even heard rumours of redundancies on the cards."

Cindy looks worried "We may lose our jobs! I'm the last

one in so probably the first one out. Do you really think that could happen, Marion?"

"It's a possibility, but don't worry about it darlin'. This company's been going for zillions of years, we'll get through, we always do."

I stare up at the glorious newcomer and feel the stirrings of jealously mix things up a little. I would love to power dress and converse with management at a high level. In this case, the mezzanine floor. She is looking thoughtful and the owner appears to be charming and attentive and my heart dips a little. She has respect because she deserves it. She's not content with standing in line, she wants to be at the front of it and probably went to university and everything.

They move away and Cindy sighs. "She's so lucky."

"Why?" Marion shakes her head as Cindy says enviously, "She looked like a movie star."

Gail feels obviously put out and snaps, "Well, I've seen better and anyway, we really should be getting on with our work. Richie told me that management are seriously watching us and anyone found shirking their duties will be asked to leave."

We fall silent because the only person we wish would leave is the smug bitch who last spoke and so, feeling the devil rise in me, I say with great satisfaction, "I had a date last night."

The others look at me with interest as Gail stiffens beside me. "And you're only just telling us that, spill every detail, who is he, where did you meet…?"

Marion sounds excited and I know they will help me lay this on thick because both of my friends are so angry about the Gail and Richie situation, they will want me to have my revenge.

"Well, he's rich, successful and looks like a movie star."

Gail shakes her head and rolls her eyes, which doesn't

escape my attention because she obviously thinks I'm making the whole thing up just to get back at her.

"Wow, where did you meet him?" Cindy's eyes are wide as I smile like the cat who got the cream.

"Um, Dream Beginnings."

I say the first thing that comes to mind and Gail snorts beside me and whispers under her breath, "Loser."

Ignoring her, I carry on laying it on thick. "It was so romantic. We went to a masquerade party at Luton Hoo."

"Wow, Polly, that's impressive."

I enjoy being the centre of attention and feeling their envy rather than pity for a change and say smugly, "Yes, it was very special."

"What does he do for a living?" Cindy's eyes are huge and I shrug. "Mergers and Acquisitions in London. He's home for Christmas and we've been talking and messaging online and as luck would have it, he comes from Harpenden, so this was the perfect time to meet at last."

"I'm not sure I agree with internet dating, it's a little risky, you should be careful Polly." Marion sounds worried and Gail says bitchily, "That's the only way some people get to date, Marion, you know, the desperate ones who can't find love in the normal way."

She almost purrs as she says dreamily, "I didn't tell you all about when Richie…"

"Carry on Polly." Marion is quick to cut in and I smile. "Anyway, he's quite a catch as it turns out. We danced and laughed, and I've never felt so relaxed with anyone as I do him. Goodness, he makes my past efforts look like amateurs and Richie did me a huge favour when he moved on because Miles is one hundred times better."

Marion laughs and Cindy's mouth twitches as Gail throws down her cracker and says tightly, "I need a comfort break."

41

She storms off and Marion says hopefully, "That did really happen Polly, please tell me it did and you're not just winding Gail up?"

"As a matter of fact, Marion, I'm telling the God's honest truth. Miles is fantastic and I can't wait to see him again."

"When will you, see him again, I mean?"

They hang onto my every word and I'm enjoying the experience. "I'm not sure, but soon. In fact, it can't come soon enough for me because I'm in dire need of some fun for once."

"Ladies, stop gossiping and get on with your work. Where's Gail?"

Richie heads over, looking irritated and Marion snaps, "Skiving off as usual. She visits that toilet more times than the rest of the workforce put together."

"Bullying in the workplace is a punishable offence, Marion, don't let me issue you with a written warning."

Richie glares at us before storming off, no doubt to hook up with Gail in one of the cubicles. They think we don't know what goes on when the rest of us are hard at it but *I* know. We used to meet a lot in the staff toilets for a quick moment of illicit pleasure, and I'm pretty certain they are at it most days. Once again, the tears burn as I remember what it felt like to be desired and wanted. "You're better off without him, darlin'. Miles sounds one hundred times better already."

Marion's kind voice pushes away the desperation and I nod. "He is, thanks Marion, it's just so hard seeing them every day and hearing her describe things we used to do and more. I mean, he already treats her way better than he ever did me, it doesn't make me feel good knowing that."

Marion puts her arm around me and says softly, "He was wrong for you, we could all see you were so much better than him. Don't beat yourself up about it and just be grateful it was over quickly. Imagine being saddled with the creep for life. No, you deserve more, and by the sounds of it you're heading in the right direction."

We fall silent, and only the sounds of the Christmas songs on the radio indicate what a special time of year it is. Every day in the cracker factory is Christmas, and it's hard to be excited about the season when you live with it day in day out. Strangely, my thoughts turn to the woman I saw with Mr Sullivan and I feel a ball of unhappiness bounce around inside me. I want that, I want a better life, but the problem is, I don't know the first thing about how to get it.

CHAPTER 9

*S*usie is slumped on the settee watching a movie on the Christmas channel when I head wearily home after another trying day.

She flicks off the television and says eagerly, "Come and sit down and tell me everything, how did it go, was your date nice and did you drink too much because you look awful?"

"Thanks, I'm pleased to see you too."

I sink down beside her and kick off my shoes, groaning as my toes flex in pure bliss at their freedom.

"To be honest, Suze, I had a great time. As you know, I was dreading it, but Miles, well, he was a gentleman."

"Miles, ooh, cool name. Was he old, bald, fat, thin? Put me out of my misery here."

Thinking back on the delectable Miles, I smile softly. "He was young, good looking and well spoken. He made me laugh and we had fun."

Susie looks at me in astonishment. "You lucky…"

"Don't say it, you made me go, remember. Anyway, how was the adorable Kevin, who I have yet to meet to endorse that opinion of him?"

It may be my imagination but Susie's eyes cloud over a little and she looks down, saying tightly, "It was fine, I guess."

"Hold on a minute – fine. Since when was any time spent with Kevin just – fine? Normally you gush about him for days. What happened?"

I feel a little concerned because this is unexpected and Susie says sadly, "I don't know, maybe it's me but I kind of thought he was the one. I mean, I don't offer to cook for anyone, you know that but well, we've been seeing each other for a few weeks now and to be honest, I can't keep my hands off him."

"So, what went wrong?"

"I don't know, me perhaps. It's just that I started to think and realised we only ever see each other here - at the flat."

"But what about when you met, where was that again?"

"He was a client, you know, a date for the evening. We really hit it off and I thought he really liked me. He asked to see me again and I didn't hesitate. I mean, I really thought he was the one I had been looking for. We were supposed to go out for a meal and he called and told me he had a hard day at work and could he just come here? I wanted to see him, so I agreed – of course. He was good company and even brought pizza and wine. Well, one thing led to another and well, you know."

"Yes, you can spare me the diagrams. But that was weeks ago. Why haven't you been out on any dates since?"

She shrugs. "There's always an excuse, something to make him insist on staying in. Then, yesterday, I thought it was going to change. He came around at lunchtime and seemed different somehow."

"What, good different, or alarm bells ringing different?"

"Good different. He told me he loved me and I deserved more. He wanted to make me happy and he had a special evening lined up for us. I thought we were finally going out, but he told me I should cook. Set the table and make it special because he had something he wanted to ask me."

"Weird. Why not take you out to a fancy restaurant, why the flat all the time?"

Susie's eyes brim with tears and she says in a whisper, "I was such a fool, Polly."

I can feel my blood boiling before she even speaks because it's certain he did, or said something to upset my best friend and I'm ready to go to war on her behalf and say tightly, "Tell me."

"I made such an effort; you know I did. I even tried to cook something and got the recipe from the internet. Autumn lamb with baby vegetables. It was awful. I couldn't work out the oven temperature, and it ended up being cremated rather than slowly roasted. By the time he arrived, he was two minutes before the fire engine. He helped me disconnect the smoke alarm and put out the fire and agreed we should order a takeaway instead. That wasn't the only disaster though."

"What happened?"

I can't wait for the punchline because one thing's for sure, if I ever see this Kevin, a big dose of my mind is the only thing I'll be giving him and Susie thumps the cushion beside her and says angrily, "I'm such a fool. He had a proposition for me alright and I never saw it coming. As it turns out, Kevin Potter is already married with his first baby on the way. He told me he had arranged an escort because he was seriously having doubts about his relationship and wanted to see if he was attracted to another woman. Well, it turns out he was, and yet how could he leave his wife with a new baby on the way? So, he thought of a plan where I would rent an apartment near to the unhappy couple and provide refuge when he needed it. He could see me more and yet stay close to his family – for the baby's sake, apparently. Then, when the child went to university, he would be free."

"Are you kidding me?"

I stare at her in horror and she glares at me angrily. "Maybe not the last part, but I'm in no doubt he would never leave his wife. What a sleazebag. I couldn't believe what I was hearing. He thought I was some kind of prostitute who would jump at the chance to be a kept woman at his beck and call."

"What did you do?"

"I threw the Chinese at him and told him to get out before I called his wife and did the job for him. I never wanted to see him again, and if I did, I would maim him. He wouldn't be able to father any more children after I laid my hands on him, and then he left. Just like that, with a disappointed shake of the head as if I was being unreasonable and told me to think about it and he would be in touch. Can you believe the cheek of the man? I can't believe I fell for his lies."

She puts her face in her hands and begins to cry, and my heart seethes with rage for the elusive Kevin Potter.

I rub circles on her back and whisper words of sympathy because this was me sitting where she is just a few weeks ago. I know the pain of a broken relationship when it's not had time to die of natural causes and my heart aches for my friend.

After a while, she stops and sinks back on the settee and says wearily. "Well, I hope your evening was better than mine. It sounds as if it was. Do you think you'll sign up with the agency, it can be fun?"

"Well, as it happens, I am already fully booked."

"What?"

Her eyes are wide as she stares at me in disbelief and I grin. "As it turned out, he also had a proposition for me and it is mutually beneficial."

"Go on."

"Well, he needs someone to pretend to be his girlfriend to get his family off his back over Christmas. Apparently, they keep on trying to set him up with women and he's tired of it. This way it keeps them off his back and I get to boast about my new 'boyfriend' at work. It's a winning situation that suits us both."

"That's amazing, is he going to pay you?"

Feeling the distaste on my tongue at the thought of being paid for my company, I try to be diplomatic. "He's paying my fee to charity. Between us, it didn't feel right earning money like that and I did like him, it just made me happier to think something who needs it more would benefit from my adventures."

"Polly…"

"Yes." I look at her anxiously because I have a feeling she's about to tell me something terrible which will destroy the smug halo that has settled around my heart.

"Don't take this the wrong way, but do you trust him? I mean, men will say anything to win your trust, I should know. In having an arrangement outside the agency, you won't be protected. What if he's making this story up and wants to get you on your own? It seems a bit too good to be true if I'm honest and you don't know the first thing about him."

"I know that I like him." The words hang in the air and even I know how silly they sound. *Like him*. I do and can't wait to spend more time with him, but what if Susie's right? He could be a murderer, or rapist, and I'm falling right into his trap. Why did he insist on wearing a mask when we met? Was it to disguise his identity from the CCTV cameras and fellow guests? Will he arrange to meet up and take me to a secluded spot and murder me?

Susie looks concerned and I feel my heart plunge into

freefall. She's right. I'm a fool because nobody is as perfect as Miles Carlton, if that's his real name. I have my serious doubts on that and yet…

I stare at the paint that's peeling on the ceiling, reminding me we need to contact the landlord about a few broken things and say in a small voice, "That makes two of us."

"What do you mean?"

"Two fools who believe their lies. I think you're right, Susie. Why would someone like that want to spend time with me unless he wanted to murder me?"

"I didn't say that, it's not what I meant."

"Maybe not, but it's the truth, it all adds up. Fake names, a costume that hides his identity, some lame story about needing a girlfriend for Christmas, and I was the fool who told him I had no plans for Christmas so nobody would miss me."

"No plans." Susie looks at me sharply and I shrink inside. "What do you mean, no plans? I thought you were going to your mum's."

"I changed my mind."

"Because of him - Miles?"

"No." I sigh heavily. "Because I hate Christmas, if you must know."

"But nobody hates Christmas, it's against the law."

"Then lock me up and throw away the key. I've always hated Christmas because I never understood what the fuss was about. It was just another day when I had to put on a smart dress and pretend to be pleased with the latest offering from the sale section at the local supermarket. I was always the one on the edge, the child nobody really wanted. I was given presents of things that never interested me but were chosen because they were 'on offer'. I was never asked for my letter to Santa and there wasn't even a named stocking hanging from the radiator like my mum's new children take for granted. I was an afterthought, a duty and a cuckoo in the nest. She was so busy playing at being super stepmum, she forgot she had an actual blood relative who could really use some motherly love."

My voice is devoid of emotion because I gave up caring years ago. It's just become a fact of my childhood that made me realise I would never place my own children in that same situation. I want the world for mine, where all I had was the scraps. Maybe that's why I believed Miles so readily. I wanted to feel needed for once and fell for his lies. I feel like such a fool and stand, saying wearily, "I'll make us both a nice cup of tea while you consult the Uber oracle. Choose something you fancy, I really don't feel like cooking tonight."

CHAPTER 10

We are in the middle of pizza and 'I'll Save You This Christmas' when the phone rings. I don't recognise the number and say sleepily, "Polly Proudlock speaking."

A soft laugh floats down the line and my heart starts thumping.

"And there I was thinking I was calling Pussy Galore. What's this, another one of your many identities my 00 friend?"

"Miles."

My voice sounds a little light and breathless, and Susie rolls her eyes and silences the sound on the tv before looking at me with interest.

I can feel myself blushing as he says huskily, "Thanks for a lovely evening yesterday, I was hoping we could arrange another one."

Susie shakes her head and I say with a slight quiver to my voice, "What did you have in mind?"

She rolls her eyes and beats her head with her fist and stares at me pointedly, and I just lower my voice and turn slightly away. "I have tickets to the local ice skating show for tomorrow night. My father's taking my mother, it's an annual event and insisted I bring my new girlfriend to meet them."

"Meet your parents!"

Susie almost collapses in shock as he laughs softly. "It sounds worse than it is, but we need to put on a good show. I have a feeling my mum knows I'm up to something and I need to head her off at the pass. So, will you be my date, Polly Galore? Shall I pick you up at 7?"

Pick me up! Looking around the flat, I stare at Susie in horror. He's definitely not coming here - ever because if he insists on staying in just one night, I'll never forgive him. No, I'm not falling into the same trap as my broken-hearted friend, so I say firmly, "It's fine, text me the address and I'll meet you there."

"Are you sure, I hate to think of you having to make your own way?"

"I'm fine, I'm a grown up, I can use public transport without a minder."

I feel a little bad at the briskness of my tone, but I'm drawing a line in the snow and forbidding him to cross it. So, he sighs and says softly, "Then I'll do as you say, but I will not let you use public transport to get home. I'll drop you back, I insist."

"Fine, we'll discuss that later."

He laughs and says with a hint of triumph in his voice, "Look out for my text, Miss Moneypenny. It will self-destruct in three seconds."

He cuts the call and I find myself smiling at the phone. Idiot.

Susie shakes her head. "This is bad."

"What is?"

"That look on your face, you like him."

"As a friend." I roll my eyes and stare at her pointedly as she zaps the sound back up and Christmas music fills the room. "Keep telling yourself that, babe."

We turn our attention back to the movie, but I can't concentrate. Images of Miles invade the screen and I feel a shiver of expectation that has no business being there. This is business, purely business, and I must remember that because if I think it's anything different, I will only end up disappointed.

By the time tomorrow night comes, I have exhausted every outfit in my meagre wardrobe and watched every YouTube video on making a good impression. If it was just us, I would happily wear something a little cooler and more fashionable, but his parents. What do you wear to meet someone's parents? Richie never bothered to take me to meet his and mine wouldn't care if I said I was marrying Prince Harry. They would probably just be glad I was off their hands and probably tied up in regal duties for the foreseeable future.

Susie watches me from the open doorway and shakes her head. "Why are you stressing about this, it's only a job, what does it matter what they think of you?"

"It matters to me."

She shrugs and heads inside, armed with two mugs of steaming tea.

"So, what's the plan, I mean, you're watching the show, I get that, but what about afterwards, are you expected to suffer a meal with them, or a post-show drink in a swanky hotel bar?"

"Who knows?" I feel the butterflies tearing me up inside and try to remember how to breathe. Susie smirks and I say angrily, "If you must know, I'm dreading this because all my life I've been terrified of people like them."

"Like who?"

"People like Miles's family. You know, people with money, nice houses, cars and foreign holidays. I'm guessing they both play golf – well. I expect they're into sailing and après-ski twice a year. People like that drive Range Rovers and belong to country clubs. What if they ask me what I do for a living? Factory working stuffing crackers doesn't really shout success, does it? What if they ask me what school I went to and how much the fees were per term? The local state school wouldn't seem a good move, not to mention the fact I qualified for free school meals and was forced into every after-school club going, even the breakfast one."

"They sound terrible."

"I know. It's a stressful problem that I can't wrap my head around. I wouldn't be surprised if they start speaking in French or German half way through the evening."

"Now you're delirious."

"Oh Suze, what am I going to do? I just don't measure up."

I flop onto the bed and Susie shouts, "Just one cotton picking minute my girl, what if *they* don't measure up? From the sounds of it, if they are anything like you describe, who wants to know them, anyway? Admittedly, you paint an attractive picture of a lifestyle I would kill for, but if I did ever reach those dizzy heights, I would never look down on those struggling behind me. Life's a game babe, some of us are just better at it than most. They are no different, just privileged, or lucky. If you want to be the best person you can be, be yourself and they will love you regardless of how much money you have, or what you wear. Miles wouldn't ask you if he didn't think you could pull it off anyway, so go out there and knock them dead."

Her words do the trick and I smile gratefully. "Thanks, Suze, you're right. I am magnificent."

We share a grin and she raises her mug of tea to mine. "Show them what a great girl you are, they will love you and if they don't, it's because they are obviously mad."

With a deep breath, I apply some lipstick and look at my reflection in the mirror. The girl who looks back at me looks absolutely terrified and I'm not sure if it's because of meeting Miles's parents, or the man himself, because ever since I was Robin to his Batman, I haven't managed to shake him from my mind.

CHAPTER 11

*M*iles arranged to meet me at a pub near to the show venue and it feels a little strange pushing my way through the crowd to meet a man and his parents who are strangers to me. The air is thick with excitement and alcohol as the customers take refuge from a cold winter's night in December. The noise of conversation creates a backdrop of laughter and life, and I love seeing a roaring fire in an old inglenook at the far end of the pub. Nobody cares that a lone woman weaves her way through groups of people all out to have a good time, and I look anxiously for any indication that my date is here. What if I don't recognise him, after all, he was wearing a mask when I last saw him? I might walk right past him and not even know it.

Feeling a little silly, I try to look as if I'm comfortable being here and it's only when my gaze lands on a lone man propping up the bar, that the relief hits me. It's him. I just know it.

Making the most of the fact he hasn't seen me, I stare at him with a hunger that has no reason being there. He is every bit as gorgeous as I remember. Gone is the cape and in its place is a padded jacket, with a cashmere scarf tied casually around his neck.

His dark hair is cut short which must make his ears cold and he stares broodingly into a pint of what looks like lager. He is wearing jeans and Timberland boots and looks as if he is way more comfortable being here than me, and my heart races just a little faster as I wait for him to notice me. Like in a movie, he sweeps his eyes stage right and stares right at me. Then recognition dawns on his face as I approach. I can't help smiling broadly as he raises his eyes and smiles, apparently happy to see me, which makes me feel relieved. Thank God.

As I draw closer, he stands a little straighter and catches the attention of the barman and says in his deep, sexy voice, 'What can I get you?'

"Oh. White wine please, a small house one will be fine."

The barman nods and heads off and Miles grins. "I'm glad you made it. I wondered if you might had second thoughts and leave me here."

"Why would I? I mean, we made a deal and I never go back on my word."

"That's good to hear, I'm impressed."

For a moment we just stare at each other a little awkwardly. Without the mask to hide behind, it appears that we are both a little lost and then luckily my drink arrives and I dive on it as if it's a lifeline. Grateful for some alcohol to give me false courage, I look around.

"Are your parents here?"

"No, they're meeting us there. I thought we should arrive together, you know, like a boyfriend and girlfriend would."

"Of course."

I take a sip of my wine as I feel the nerves return, and he smiles reassuringly.

"They will love you, relax."

"Are you sure about that? I mean, they must think it a little strange."

"What?"

"Well, me suddenly making an appearance. What have you told them?"

"That we met online and have been cyber dating for months."

"Cyber dating?"

He laughs. "Yes, you know, FaceTime, Skype, all that. I also told them we met up in London when you came down for a convention."

My mouth goes dry and I lick my lips nervously.

"A convention. What sort of convention?"

"It's ok, I was very vague and just glossed over it and they dropped the subject. Just tell them what you want to, they'll believe anything."

He grins. "I'm guessing you are in for quite a surprise when you meet them. You've probably formed your own opinion already and I'll be interested to see if it's right or not."

I groan inside. If my opinion turns out correct, I'm in trouble, so I just smile mysteriously and take another gulp of my wine.

The pubs filling up and the noise is deafening, so much so that it's hard to hear him and after a while, he just sets his glass down and leans in. "We should go, the show starts at 7.30 and we need to grab a cab, not an easy thing to do on a cold December night."

My heart beats a little faster as I follow closely behind him as we make our way out of the warm and brightly lit pub. If I could, I would stay because it's safe here. It's just Miles and me and a horde of strangers; nobody to judge me and find me lacking. I have a feeling Miles's parents will and as always, I feel as if I don't measure up and am punching above my weight.

Luckily, Miles manages to flag down a cab almost immediately and we are soon safely inside a vehicle that smells a little musty, heading the short distance to see Frozen on Ice.

Miles appears in a relaxed mood and says good naturedly, "So, Polly Galore, how have things been since our last adventure?"

"Good thanks, how about you, it must be nice being home if you live away most of the time?"

"I wouldn't say nice exactly. Familiar, interesting maybe, but not nice."

"What's it like, living in London, it always seems a little scary to me?"

"I love it." He smiles and says with animation. "As soon as I could, I moved there. Luckily, I managed to secure a good job after university at a top London bank. The money I earned enabled me to rent a small studio flat, but it's all I need. The work is hard and demanding, but London is a place that is so invigorating. I love the atmosphere and the fast pace of life. I have many friends and we work and play hard."

I smile, but inside a sinking feeling reminds me how temporary all of this is. Miles Carlton is a man who lives a very different life to mine and as soon as the snow melts, will be heading back to his exciting life, leaving me right back where I started. Maybe I should just enjoy the moment and embrace it. Perhaps I should run with this and make a memory so amazing I won't even believe it myself. I will look back on it as the time fate took me out of my comfort zone and I lived on the edge.

Luckily, he doesn't ask me any awkward questions about my own sad and boring life and we are soon pulling up outside the venue. My heart sinks when I see a long line of people queuing outside, stamping their feet and shivering against the bitter wind and light dusting of snow on the pavement outside.

Miles pays the cab and I say nervously, "I hope I don't mess this up."

To my surprise, he takes my gloved hand and gives it a little squeeze. "You'll be fine, don't worry, my parents are good company and you don't have to impress them, they will love you regardless."

Armed with serious doubts, I leave my hand in his – for appearance's sake, of course – and head to the line.

However, rather than joining it, he propels me around the side of the building towards a rear entrance. The alley is dark and my heart rate increases as I say nervously, "Um, I thought we were going inside."

"We are, just not through the front door."

He laughs softly as I stare at him in confusion and whispers, "My dad knows the manager. He told us to head to the staff entrance and he'll put our names on the list. We can sneak in the back way and avoid waiting in the queue."

Feeling a little better, I push away the thought of him murdering me in a dark alley and just try to do as he says - relax.

It doesn't take long to reach the door and Miles pushes our way inside a stark entrance with peeling paint on the walls and just an old poster of a show from many years ago. There's a security booth to the side and Miles raps on the glass window and says loudly, "Hi, Graham Rafferty told us we could sign in here for the show. The name's Miles Carlton, plus one."

Feeling strangely happy about being referred to as Miles's plus one, I wait nervously to be thrown out on the street by the burly security guard. Instead, he nods as he consults his list and says gruffly, "Do you know where to go?"

"Not really." Miles turns and winks at me as the guard says blankly, "Through the double doors, turn right and head up the stairs. That should take you into the reception. Have your tickets ready and someone will show you to your seats."

"Great, thanks, oh, and merry Christmas."

The guard just grunts and looks back to his newspaper, and I stifle a giggle as Miles drags me at speed through the double doors.

Why does something so ordinary feel special with him? It all feels exciting and adventurous, and we've only just started. I've never been to an ice skating show and certainly never had VIP access to dodge the queues before. I could get used to this.

The dull tread of our boots sounds loud as we make our way up the stairs. The slightly subdued lighting is in direct contrast to the bright lights through the double doors that transport us into a place that's warm, inviting and exciting. The crowds are happy and laughing and there is a buzz of excitement in the room as everyone anticipates an evening of entertainment and enjoyment in a month where the weather does its best to drag everyone down.

All around us are twinkling lights and Christmas decorations, sparkling in the light, reminding us there is more excitement to come. Groups of people huddle together, laughing and greeting one another with pleasure and happiness, and I picture my usual evening spent curled up on my sofa watching other people live their lives.

This time it's me. The girl who stepped outside her comfort zone and did something completely out of character. I like where it's taking me, so far, anyway, and it feels good to be included for once. Richie never included me in anything. Like Kevin, he was happier to stay in of an evening and never treated me to a surprise show, or a meal in a fancy restaurant. He is treating Gail much better than me, and that's the part that hurts the most. Why was I not special enough to wine and dine and try to impress? Was I so desperate that I would do anything he asked, just because I felt lucky to have his attention?

My thoughts are interrupted as Miles shouts to make himself heard above the hum of conversation. "Shall we grab a drink and head off to find them?"

"Sounds good." My heart starts beating fast as I contemplate meeting his parents. At least the show will cancel out any need for conversation, but I'm still nervous. It feels a little wrong playing a part, as if I'm an imposter who has no business being here. Grateful for the Dutch courage Miles thrusts into my hand, I feel my legs shake as I follow him. What will I find when I get there and will this evening end in disaster when it started off so well?

CHAPTER 12

$\mathcal{T}$he moment of truth comes quickly and I look with surprise as we stop outside a door marked 'Box 1.' Miles goes to open it and I say nervously, "Are you sure this is the right place?"

"Yes, my caped crusader, this is Box 1 and inside are my parents, who can't wait to meet you by the way."

"But..."

Miles smiles and I just stare at him with what I'm sure is a lustful look. Can he get any more attractive because Miles Carlton is surely an act of God? A man who doesn't have to try too hard and somebody us mere mortals have only heard about. The fact he's directing that powerful man stare at me is seriously hard to understand and I swallow hard as he leans down and says in a whisper, "I told you, we know a man and that counts for a lot. You'll soon realise that my parents know lots of men and if you play your cards right in life, you get to enjoy a five star one on a working man's salary. It's how you play the game that counts, not how much money you lay on the table."

I don't have time to think because he pushes open the

door and I see two people look up with interest as we venture inside.

They look ordinary enough. An attractive woman who looks chic and elegant with a kind smile and a twinkle in her eye, is holding the hand of an attractive man, distinguished and handsome with greying hair to his temples and a cheeky smile. Far from looking at me with horror, they are merely looking at me with interest and I breathe a sigh of relief. First hurdle over.

Miles welcomes his parents with enthusiasm, which tells me that he loves them very much and I watch with a tinge of envy as they hug him warmly and squeeze him for just a moment longer than is customary.

Then they look past him to me and his mother smiles broadly and says in a thick cockney accent, "Look at you, you must be Polly, come in darlin' and sit next to me, I've been dying to meet you, haven't I babe?"

She looks at her husband, who smiles with interest and laughs jovially. "Hasn't stopped talking about you since Miles told us he was bringing a plus one. Pleased to meet you Poll, darlin', I'm Elvis, Miles's dad and this is Pauline my better half."

Blinking in surprise, I find myself pulled into a warm embrace and almost lifted off my feet as Elvis launches himself on me a little too exuberantly. His wife does the same and I feel the fear get up and leave as she pulls me down beside her and says happily, "Sit next to me, babe and tell me everything. I'm dying to hear your life story."

Miles laughs and sits beside his dad and says with laughter in his voice, "Go easy on her mum, I don't want you to scare her away."

A delicious feeling of warmth floods my body at his words that I immediately push aside because it has no business being there. Miles doesn't mean anything he says, and I'd be wise to remember that.

Pauline thrusts a bag of sweets at me and says brightly, "Fancy a Haribo, Polly, have as many as you want. I've got three more packets in my bag."

"Thanks, gummy bears, my favourites."

Cramming the chewy sweets into my mouth, I feel a lot better than earlier. Miles was right, his parents are completely different to what I imagined. They look well to do, but they are no different than me inside. Thank God, normal people. Well, at least on the outside.

Pauline looks at me with a twinkle in her eye and says with interest, "So, darlin', what do you do for a job?"

Feeling myself blush a little, I say dismissively, "Um, production."

"Really, what do you produce?"

"Christmas items, crackers to be precise."

Pauline looks ecstatic, which surprises me a little and turns to her husband who is sitting behind her. "Elvis, Polly makes crackers, can you believe that, we have so much in common."

Elvis laughs loudly, "Bloody hell, Pauline, you must think Christmas has come early. Don't miss the show and chew the poor girl's ear off."

I catch Miles's eye and he looks amused and once again I feel bad. They're being so nice, they probably think I'm some kind of super-powered executive like Miss Constable in her smart power suits and styled hair, not the minion stuffing crackers, earning just above the minimum wage with no business being in an executive box about to watch the hottest show in town, where tickets are selling for five times their face value on eBay.

Pauline says with excitement. "You know, I dabble in

crackers myself, babe. I love making my own and sometimes I make a few to sell on my Etsy store. We must compare notes and see if I can get any ideas from a professional. Here, Miles…" She turns and smiles at her son before adding, "Bring Polly around for lunch tomorrow and I'll show her my craft room. Make it early so I get some time to bend her ear on all things crackers."

Miles fixes me with a look that would melt the Arctic, and I swear my toes actually curl as I try to look unaffected. "Sure, are you up for that, Polly?"

"Oh, um, yes, thank you, if you're sure it's not too much trouble."

Elvis rolls his eyes. "You may regret saying yes, babe, once Pauline gets you in that tatt room, you may not make it out alive."

"Take no notice of him, Polly, he's just miffed because I spend more time in there than he does his garage, which let me tell you, needs a serious tidy up. It's like walking into a room after the burglars have left."

"Only because of all your rubbish. Why do I still have twenty boxes of Christmas decorations in there when I built you that shed in the garden?"

"That's my studio, not a dumping ground. Honestly Elvis, just board out the rafters and put them up there if they're upsetting you."

She leans in and whispers, "As if he ever will, he's all talk and no action like most men. Love to complain but don't do anything about it. Word of advice babe, don't let Miles get complacent, keep him on his toes and demand the world. Always keep something back and don't ever let them think they've got you."

I nod, but I'm becoming increasingly miserable inside. They are so nice and we are pretending to be something we're not. Now I've met Miles's parents, I can't understand why he's doing this. They will be so upset when they discover we've lied to them, and I'm not sure I can go through with this. Miles will have to find someone else to play this part because increasingly, I'm coming to the conclusion that it can't be me.

The show starts and I turn my attention to that instead. Despite how uncomfortable I feel, I am interested to see the most popular show in town. I've seen the adverts and watched the cast interviewed on the local news and everyone's talking about it at work. Nobody has actually been to see it though, which makes me smile as I picture their faces on Monday morning when I gloat about it on the production line.

The usual theatre has been transformed for the occasion and looks like a glittering ice palace. Somehow, they have transformed the stage into an ice rink and the lights bounce off the ice, making it sparkle and dance in the blue light. As the music starts, I feel my heart beat with excitement. I have never been to a show before, let alone an ice one. This truly is how the other half live and I could get used to it. Never having been given the chance to experience things like this for myself, it means a lot and despite the fact I feel so uncomfortable at being here on false pretences, I am determined to make the most of the occasion.

As the lights dim, I try to forget that I am playing a part myself and turn my attention to the stage and fall in love with the magic of Frozen all over again.

THE INTERVAL ARRIVES and as the lights come on, I turn to Pauline and smile happily. "That was amazing."

She nods. "I know, I just can't get enough of it. Did Miles tell you we come here every year and have done since he was three years old?"

Elvis snorts, "It's why we know the manager so well, we've paid for this box over the years, so it's no wonder he lets us have it at no extra charge."

Pauline nods. "Such a lovely man. Elvis plays squash with him twice a week. Do you play any sports, Polly?"

"Not really, I should though."

Pauline nods. "Yes, it's important to your health. You should play with Miles, sport I mean, and not the games I'm sure he has in mind."

She winks and I want to curl up in a ball as her meaning is obvious. In fact, I feel a little hot under the collar just imagining the sort of games Miles likes to play and find myself wishing I could experience that first-hand. Then it gets even worse as he leans down and whispers loudly, "Polly loves playing games, don't you, darling? She's actually really good at it too."

Pauline rolls her eyes and shares a look with her husband, who shakes his head laughing.

"Miles never stops playing games, Polly. He has made it his life's work to send us to an early grave and claim his inheritance."

Pauline squeals with laughter. "Do you remember the time he put an eye mask over you when you were sleeping and you woke up thinking you'd turned blind in the night. I haven't laughed so much in months hearing the fear in your voice."

What the...

I stare at them in disbelief as Elvis laughs loudly. "I remember when he made that fake wall with paper and drew graffiti on it when we were out one day. I thought Pauline was going to have a heart attack when she returned to find her newly decorated hallway looking like something from the ghetto."

They all laugh and I stare at them in astonishment as

Miles grins and shakes his head. "It's only because you told me half term had been cancelled and made me get up and ready for school and walk half an hour in the rain, only to find the school closed. Then I had to walk back again, only to find you both laughing when I got there."

"It's character building, son, it's made you who you are today."

Miles winks at me as Pauline giggles, "What about the time we made out we won the lottery. Your dad went ballistic and invited all the neighbours in and cracked open that champagne he's been saving for your wedding."

Elvis groans. "Don't remind me, it was only after I booked the appointment at the Ferrari garage you told me it was all a laugh. I was gutted, Polly, as I'm sure you can imagine."

As they continue to swap stories, it all falls into place. This family love nothing more than playing practical jokes on each other and I am just another elaborate one. As I listen, I find myself laughing in horror at some of the things they've done, and by the time the second half of the show starts, I have a deeper understanding of how this family gets their kicks. Now I understand, I don't feel so bad, but there is a large part of me that still feels wrong about this. I'm beginning to think that when they discover the deception, it will only be me left feeling rattled by the whole experience because the more time I spend with Miles and his family, the more I wish this wasn't a lie and I never want this month to end.

CHAPTER 13

"*Y*our parents are nice; you must feel very proud."

Miles nods and says with a slight edge to his voice. "Thanks, Polly."

"For what?"

"For going along with this."

I nod but my heart sinks and I can't help saying, "I feel bad though."

He sighs heavily and says in a slightly husky voice, "Me too."

We are sitting in a pub just around the corner from the theatre after having waved Pauline and Elvis off as they head home. Miles offered to buy them dinner, but they refused because Elvis has an early start on the golf course and Pauline is knee deep in Christmas shit, as she put it so eloquently.

We are due to visit for Sunday lunch and once again I feel bad about that.

Miles is also unusually quiet and as we nurse two large brandies by the open fire, he suddenly leans forward and directs a scorching look at me that makes the fire seem cold in comparison.

"You must be wondering why I'm doing this."

"Well, now you mention it…"

To my surprise, he takes my hand and looks so sad I think I hold my breath. What is he going to say?

"The thing is, ever since Kate, things haven't been the same. She drove a wedge between us, and now there's a tense atmosphere at home where there never was before. Freddie can't look me in the eye and when he does, it's with a guilty look on his face. Mum tries to pretend it never happened and Jessica, our sister, is bitter about the whole thing and thinks it's helpful to cyber stalk Kate and tell us every detail of what she's getting up to. I just thought if I brought somebody home this Christmas, somebody to show them I've moved on and left Kate and the whole sorry business behind me, things would get back to normal. They would be focused on you, not the past, and I would get my family back."

As I stare at him in shock, I feel the compassion replacing my guilt and squeeze his hand a little in sympathy. He smiles apologetically and sighs. "I know you found that hard, to be honest I did too. I hate lying to my parents but couldn't think of another way."

"But haven't you met anyone since, I mean, dated for real?"

I hate the jealously that my words cause to flare inside me and Miles shakes his head. "I've dated quite a lot as it happens. Girls that looked the same as Kate and ones that looked completely different. All ages, all shapes and all types, but none of them measured up. None of them lasted past a third date because they weren't her."

"Oh."

His words crush me as I realise, he still loves her. Is it

possible to hate a person you've never met because I'm hating this Kate with a passion right now and not because of what she did to the man holding my hand so tightly? It's because of the jealousy I feel inside, wishing that he loved me like that. Once again, I feel bad and say hesitatingly, "You want her back?"

Miles looks at me in surprise and then laughs bitterly. "At first maybe, but as the months went on, I grew to hate her. Thinking of the damage she caused to me and my family was like a physical pain and if she came crawling on her hands and knees and begged me to take her back, I wouldn't."

"But you said…"

"They weren't her." He laughs.

"What I meant was they weren't a person I wanted to spend the rest of my life with. They weren't that perfect dream I had when I was part of a couple, planning our future and supposedly in love. I loved the feeling of being with the person you were always meant to find and no longer suffered the uncertainty of looking for your perfect companion. You see, Polly, I had a happy childhood. My parents are amazing – the best in fact and set the bar high. If I manage to find my soulmate like they did, I would consider myself the richest man alive. I thought I had that with Kate, but she, as it turned out, thought differently. She destroyed my trust in love, and I suppose that's why I thought I needed to shake things up a little. Have the appearance of love with none of the emotions it brings to the table. Show my parents, my family, that I've moved on and now they must too. Restore the family dynamic and heal the rift my relationship caused. My parents would stop worrying and my brother would be able to move on, happy that things worked out fine in the end. My sister could direct her anger to something less raw and I would be free to pretend none of it had happened."

"That's so sad."

"Excuse me, why is wanting to make it all better, sad?"

"Because you're lying to the most important person in your life – you. You will hide behind a veil of smiles and light relief, but inside you will still hurt. You need to deal with your own pain before you can hope to repair the damage she caused to your family. Only you can heal Miles Carlton and pretending everything is fine and dandy means you are lying to yourself as much as your family."

He drops my hand and leans back, the firelight flickering in his eyes as they flash with what appears to be anger. I see the bitterness in his expression as he snaps. "I'll be fine. I just want everything to get back to normal and that will heal the wound inside."

For a moment we just sip our brandy and I think about how the atmosphere has intensified as a result of our conversation. Miles is no longer the light-hearted joker I have grown accustomed to, and in his place is a tortured man trying to give his family the best Christmas present he can – his happiness. Although I understand his reasons behind this, I'm not sure I agree with it and open my mouth to withdraw from my part in this whole charade, but he fixes me with a hard look and says quickly, "Don't say it."

"Say what? Are you a psychic now?"

He laughs and a little of the tension leaves his eyes as he says huskily, "Don't you leave me too, Polly. This may have started as a business arrangement, but I like your company. Please stick around and be my partner in crime. I mean, you are the Robin to my Batman after all, and where would the caped crusader be without his sidekick? Give me a little longer and I'll work it out, please don't give up on me just yet."

"Ok."

The fool inside me speaks up before the rational part of me can shut this deal down. I am furious with my own lack of control because I know I should walk away – no, run away fast. This isn't right, but I can't help how I feel. Miles needs me and actually I need him more because just having spent two evenings with him is enough for me to know that I have never felt as happy as I have with him my entire life and it's the selfish part of me that wants to cling onto this feeling and run with it fast.

Maybe it's not right and maybe I should come clean to his parents, but I want to see them again and I want to see Pauline's craft room of tatt. I want to meet his brother and sister and see what a proper family who love one another with a fierceness that must be hard to live with at times, is like. But most of all, I want to spend more time with Miles because he is something I never thought I'd experience. Is Miles my Christmas present to myself this year because it certainly feels that way to me? Is he a Christmas miracle that I never saw coming? So, I decide to give him one last date. I'll do dinner tomorrow and worry about the effects of it on Monday. This is my weekend and I'm going to seize it and hold on tight because opportunities like this don't come along that often - not to me, anyway. So, as I settle back in my seat and take a sip of my brandy, I push away the part of me that is telling me this is wrong on every level.

CHAPTER 14

"**W**hat are you going to do?"

Groaning, I put my hands over my face and shake my head. "I really don't know. On the one hand, I should tell Miles enough is enough and it's not fair on anyone."

"And the other…?"

"I don't want to walk away from something that is the most exciting thing to ever happen to me. I mean, I really like his parents. They are so much fun and were so sweet to me. Would it really hurt if I pretended a little more, I mean, it is for charity, after all?"

Susie looks worried and sits beside me on the bed. "Maybe you should just play along and then look back on a fabulous Christmas, but this isn't you, Polly. You're the most righteous person I know, and I mean that in a good way. I have a horrible feeling that the only person getting hurt in this is you because I know you rather well as it happens."

I stare at her in surprise and she shakes her head. "You like him, Miles, I mean. It's written all over your face and I'm scared you'll get hurt."

"Don't be ridiculous."

"I'm not and you know it. Just think it over and maybe go for lunch tomorrow and then make your decision after that. To be honest, I wish I'd never suggested it in the first place."

She stands and says rather grumpily, "Well, at least one of us is having a good time, I suppose."

Feeling a little bad, I say with concern, "Any news on Kevin?"

"He's called several times, but I haven't picked up. I can't, Polly. I'm no home wrecker and certainly not happy about being somebody's mistress. No, I'm getting back on the wagon and escorting a business man from Sunderland to the Hoo tomorrow night at some fancy pants dinner. Strictly above board and just what the doctor ordered."

"So, you're still happy to do the job then?" I feel a little worried for my friend because even I can see this is a bad decision. She should be looking for a normal job with normal people, not being wined and dined by faceless strangers and judged because of it.

Shrugging, she heads to the door. "I've got to get my kicks from somewhere, you know. Maybe after Christmas I'll rethink my life plan, but I can't do it now. Christmas is a busy time and I'm up for earning lots of money before I hang up my little black book."

As I snuggle down in my bed, hearing the rain lashing against the glass of the window, I shiver a little. Things are becoming increasingly complicated for both of us, and it's a result of that escort business. If I had never gone, I would never have met Miles which would be a very bad thing. Then again, as soon as Christmas ends, he will hot foot it back to London, leaving me to start planning for next Christmas in a perpetual Groundhog Day. Is this really what my life is, doing the same boring routine every day? Is that why I have thrown caution to the wind and seized an opportunity that should never have arisen?

I think I fall asleep with a thousand troubled thoughts jostling for pole position in my mind. What I need is a Christmas miracle, no, two Christmas miracles, because if I get one, I want one for my friend.

I'M HAVING a severe wardrobe crisis and my bedroom resembles a charity shop after a hurricane ripped through it. Not one item of my meagre clothing collection has been left unattended as I desperately search for something chic and yet casual to wear to lunch with Pauline and Elvis.

Susie is no help because she has gone Christmas shopping with Jonathan from downstairs. He's such a great shopping companion because he knows where all the secret sales are and when you're on a budget, you need all the help you can get. Deciding to ask him to take me thrift shop clothes shopping as a matter of urgency, I finally decide on a simple red dress – very festive – paired with a pink scarf and red shoes. The best coat I have is a black charity shop find and the only hat I possess is of the bobble variety, which makes me look slightly ridiculous.

As I stare at the waiflike creature looking back at me in the haunted mirror – called that because we discovered it in a skip off Lincoln street, outside a house where a woman is rumoured to have met an untimely death, I feel an ache in my heart as I see my reflection staring back at me.

Apart from Susie, I have no one. My parents haven't even bothered to call for weeks now and haven't asked me to spend Christmas with them, although in my dad's case it would involve jetting off to Thailand, or somewhere in the east. Mum is planning the perfect wholesome Christmas with her third new family, pretending to be Kirstie from Kirstie's handmade Christmas, leaving me twiddling my thumbs in Slip End.

Even Suze is going home and it's at times like this, my situation slaps me in the face - hard. I'm all alone and have been for some time now. Friends are no substitute for family, although they are preferable most of the time. I want my own family to be close, like Miles's family. Who wouldn't want that?

A quick glance at the clock on the wall makes me push aside any unhappiness I'm feeling and grab my bag and head for the door. I'm meeting Miles in the Frog and Rhubarb, despite the fact he tried to get my address so he could pick me up. Something is making me hold back from giving out personal information. What if things go wrong and I need to escape? The last thing I want is him knowing where I live. Security is my number one priority, which makes what I've just done a complete surprise. This isn't like me – at all. Maybe it should be though because I like who I've become because it appears that nobody liked the old Polly Proudlock anyway and that includes me.

CHAPTER 15

"*P*olly, over here."

Once again, the pub is heaving, as it normally is most Sunday afternoons and I see Miles propping up the bar in the corner of the room.

I manage to push my way through the crowd and love the way his eyes light up as he sees me approach and genuinely looks as happy to see me as I am him.

"I got you a white wine for the road, is that ok?"

"Great, thanks."

He grabs the two drinks and says loudly, "I think it's quieter through here, we'll have these and go."

I'm not sure how he does it but we manage to find a small table in an alcove that has been freshly vacated and I gratefully sit on the worn cotton cushion that has certainly seen better days.

The noise subsides a little and Miles says with relief, "Thank god, this place must be a gold mine. Look at these people, don't they have homes to go to?"

"It's Sunday, Miles, it's law that you must go to the pub, don't they follow the letter of the law in London?"

"It's all wine bars and gastro pubs there. Much more civilised with tables booked and everything."

"Sounds boring, I don't think I'll visit."

I grin to take the sting from my words and he looks at me intently. "I would love to show you London, Polly. I'm guessing it would be very different to how you imagine it."

Loving the image his words present, I say with interest, "Tell me about it."

"It's special. Yes, there are the usual tourist areas and corporate parts, but it's the little cobbled streets set behind the bright lights that fascinate me. The old buildings that could tell a fancy story and the layers of tradition and history that are absorbed with the dirt into bricks and mortar that has been around for centuries. Slightly shabby doors that lead to cellars of hidden treasures. Cosy bars and restaurants that only the locals know about. Nightclubs and bars with a strict 'members only' policy and amazing tea rooms hidden beneath the busy streets above. Even the name places hold meaning, and if you troubled to Google them, you would discover a rich history that has long been forgotten. Strange little traditions and ceremonies known by a select few that bring the city alive and give it depth, where the bright lights of the shopping areas dress it in shallowness. No, I prefer Old London, the one the public rarely gets to see, that's why I love it there."

He is speaking and looking deep into my eyes as he weaves his magical spell around my heart. His voice is husky and contains a deep emotion that makes my heart race and my knees shake. I can't tear my eyes away from his as they sparkle as he looks at me. His mouth is inches from mine as he spills his secrets and I am so far gone there is no hope left. Miles Carlton is my Kryptonite because every word from his lips has the deepest meaning. I hold on tightly to his words and commit them to memory, eager to retrieve them at a later date and remember when my heart was full.

Then he says loudly, "Good grief, look at the time, mum will be sending out a search party, are you good, Polly?"

Quickly, I take a huge gulp of wine and cough, "Sure."

I follow him from the pub like an adoring puppy. I can pretend all I like, but I already know I will do anything he asks. This whole adventure will only be over when he says it is, and if I could ask for anything for Christmas, it would be to hold on to him for a little longer.

MILES DRIVES a neat little sports car that makes me green with envy. I can't even afford a moped and must make do with the bus and train. He has leather seats and they are heated to add to the thrill. The engine purrs like a contented cat and as I settle in the passenger seat, I inhale the intoxicating aroma of leather mixed with a hint of citrus, courtesy of the magic tree dangling from the coat hook. Miles takes his place beside me and it feels good to be snuggled up next to him as he shifts the car into gear and heads off to Harpenden.

Feeling a little disgruntled that we won't be taking a long car journey, I just feel grateful to be here at all as he turns on the radio and sweet festive tunes fill the silence with magic.

The warm air from the heater soon takes effect and I find myself relaxing as we speed through the streets singing Silent Night at the top of our voices. Miles is good company; he has been every time I meet him and it rubs off. With him, I am carefree with no worries or hang ups. I can be whoever I want to be and I want to be someone entirely different to Polly Proudlock, cracker stuffer extraordinaire.

Everything about Miles oozes class and sophistication, so it's no surprise that he pulls into one of Harpenden's most desirable streets.

The houses here are straight out of a feature spread for Country Homes and Interiors. Sweeping drives with decorated porches, around which fairy lights are strung and glitter in the dusky light. Lunch time in midwinter is one step away from darkness and I love the way the windows sparkle with a warm glow, giving me a glimpse of the way the rich live inside. Gleaming cars stand proudly outside homes I could never afford, and I struggle to imagine how on earth Pauline and Elvis fit in here?

"What does your father do for a living, Miles?"

"He set up a cleaning business when he left school. One contract led to another, and now his company has the contracts for several supermarket chains. He employs six thousand people and covers the entire country. It's big business, Polly, and the rewards are great."

I think my mouth drops along with the penny as it all clicks into place. Carlton Cleaning Corporation, I've heard of it, everyone in the area has.

Miles says with pride. "It just goes to show what one person can achieve with a bit of foresight and a lot of hard work, I'm proud of him."

"Me too."

Miles laughs softly. "Thank you."

"I am as it happens, because who wouldn't be proud of someone who achieves so much. I may have just met him, but I can be proud of him, can't I?"

Miles nods. "You should be proud of yourself too."

"Me, why?" I stare at him in surprise.

"You made something happen, even though you would rather have been anywhere else. You helped a friend in need and who wouldn't be proud of that?"

"It was no big deal, I'm nothing to be proud of Miles. I told you I was in production, that much is true. But I'm no hotshot business woman, I stuff crackers on a production line day in day out. I get paid little over the minimum wage and can only afford to exist, not live. My family prefers to be strangers and I have a handful of friends who wouldn't fill an entire pew at the wedding I hope to have one day. My boyfriend pushed me aside for the woman who works alongside me and subsequently makes my life hell at work. This is the most fun I've had in years and it's not because of anything I've done except be somewhere I was never meant to be in the first place. Now I'm off to lie to two fantastic people to help out their son, who I kind of tolerate but still can't forgive for making me Robin and not something exciting like Cat Woman."

Miles laughs, a deep, throaty, sexy kind of laugh that sends my heart into freefall. Then he reaches across and covers my hand with his and squeezes it hard. "Well, I like you Polly Galore because you fascinate me. You are so different from anyone I've ever met and who cares how you earn your living? It's your future that counts, and I think yours will be a bright one. Trust me, I know these things, I am a superhero, after all."

He winks before needing both hands to turn the steering wheel into the driveway of a beautiful home that looks like something off a Christmas card.

"Honey, we're home."

He grins as he sprints from the car like Batman on a mission and gallantly comes and opens my car door, offering me his hand. "My dear, may I have the honour of escorting you inside."

"Idiot." I reach for his hand but can't stop the goofy grin from revealing my true feelings towards him. He is impossible not to like, and even the fact I'm about to enter the equivalent to Buckingham Palace doesn't bother me. I would go anywhere he asked because increasingly I am discovering he can do no wrong. In my eyes, anyway.

$\mathcal{P}$auline meets us as we step inside her absolutely enormous hallway and squeals, "They're here, Elvis, Miles and Polly are here."

I watch with amusement as she launches herself at Miles and squeezes him tightly and then does the same to me. Elvis laughs loudly as he joins us and says, "Leave them alone, Pauline, they haven't even got their coats off."

She steps back and grins. "Sorry guys, I just get so excited to see normal people I get a bit carried away. I mean, locked up in this house with your father can send a woman doolally."

Miles shakes his head and grins as Elvis says good-naturedly, "Come on, son, I've got a bottle of lager with your name on it in the fridge, let's leave the girls to it."

Miles looks at me apologetically as he follows his father and Pauline says with excitement, "Come on, Poll, I'll show you my tatt room. I've been longing for a kindred spirit to share my love of all things crafted, and I'm pretty sure you're that person."

As I shrug out of my coat and boots, she chatters incessantly. "I love Christmas, don't you, Poll? I mean, it's so magical and everything."

As she speaks, I notice that Christmas is all around us. On every wall, surface and window is something Christmas related and it takes my breath away. No cheap tinsel from Poundland here because this is more like Harrod's most spectacular window. The decorations are tasteful and designed to create a little piece of magic at a time when the cold weather does its best to destroy any good mood that may surface.

A twinkling forest of twigs stands proudly in the corner of their oversized hallway, and at the base of it are woodland creatures all in white. Stars and icicles hang from the ceiling and a soft white fur rug makes it appear as if we are walking on a carpet of snow. The bannisters are entwined with fairy lights and a sparkling white garland and little silver lanterns sit on every step, holding flickering candles that may be fake but look as real as the wonder in my heart.

Pauline notices my awestruck expression and smiles. "It takes me at least a week to decorate this place, but I love every minute of it. It's like rediscovering Christmas every year when those boxes come out and I unearth treasures that have taken me years to accumulate."

I have never seen the like of it before and picture our own rather shabby tree and generally scruffy decorations back at the flat. Growing up it was much the same and although my mum tried her best, she never had an eye for decoration, unlike Pauline who is obviously a professional at this.

I follow her up the sweeping staircase and notice even upstairs hasn't escaped her touch as I look in delight at the lanterns on the surfaces of little tables with more designer decorations than my budget would ever allow. I'm not sure how many rooms are on this level, but she doesn't give me time to count as we head up another staircase towards the top of the house. This level is just as big and we pass another set of rooms before she pushes open the door of a huge loft-style room that is crammed full of more craft items than Hobbycraft.

I want to dance in delight as I appreciate the groaning shelves of pure paradise from ribbons, to scraps of fabrics and glittering objects all waiting to find a home.

Set up against the far wall is a huge workstation and Pauline says, "Welcome to my happy place, Poll. I spend hours up here like Rapunzel in her tower, working away until my duties dictate otherwise. I love being here, listening to the radio and creating little homemade items that may not be the best you'll ever see but bring me pleasure."

I stare in awe at a place I would kill to own myself and say in wonder, "I love this room, you are so lucky."

My compliment obviously pleases her because she beams, "Come and see my crackers, you'll appreciate these, I'm sure."

She heads over to a shelf on the other side of the room and gingerly picks up the most delicate looking cracker I think I've ever seen and holds it out proudly for my inspection and I gasp with delight at the white organza wrapped cracker, sparkling with silver stars. She has decorated them exquisitely and wrapped huge white organza ribbons either side of the middle and attached a sparkling label. It is bigger than the ones we sell and she says proudly, "I make my own every year because I think everyone should feel special at Christmas. I select a little gift with the person in mind and a lovely chocolate to suit their personal preference. I trawl the internet and print out little poems and jokes that I hope are meaningful and funny, and the hats inside are my own special design. This gives me so much pleasure, Poll. I'm jealous that you get to surround yourself in creativity every day. It must be so fulfilling producing little pieces of magic like Santa's elves on a daily basis."

Picturing the cold, dismal factory that we stand inside on our production line, dressed in our hideous uniform, I shake my head sadly. "Unfortunately, it's nothing like you describe. When I said I worked in production, I meant just that. I stand in line on a production line, stuffing plastic magnifying glasses and other useless rubbish into the cheapest cracker that money can buy. The contents haven't changed for twenty years apparently, and I could tell you every one of the 'jokes' that just aren't funny in today's world. The people I work with are nice enough though, unless you count the woman next to me who somehow managed to steal my boyfriend and rubs my nose in it every day."

Pauline looks astonished and shakes her head. "You poor thing, I never knew. Why don't you do something about it if you hate it so much?"

"Easier said than done, Pauline. I'm not very qualified and there aren't many jobs available to people like me. It pays the bills and I'm loathe to give up a position that does that and yet…"

"You want more."

I nod miserably and she says with a hint of determination.

"Come and sit down, Poll, I think you need to hear this story."

Placing the cracker gingerly down, so as not to disturb the delicate decoration, I follow her to a velvet couch in the corner of the room and sit beside her, looking over a crafter's paradise wondering what she's about to say.

"Listen, babe, I know exactly where you're coming from because I've been there myself. Elvis and me never inherited our money. In fact, we were both brought up on a rough estate and went to the local state school that even Ofsted refused to visit."

She grins, and then a dreamy look enters her eyes as she is transported back in time.

"You know, Poll, when I met Elvis, he didn't know I existed. I was just plain little Pauline Cotton, the slightly scruffy girl from Luton who had bigger dreams than she had any right to. Elvis was *that* boy, you know, the one all the girls wanted and the boys wanted as their friend. With a name like Elvis Carlton, he could do no wrong. But he did. He was the local bad boy, full of excitement and he looked so hot in his battered leather jacket. He was so handsome and all the girls wanted to call him their boyfriend. You see, Poll, names are so powerful. It was his name that set him apart and his attitude that reeled you in. He's always been like that and it's a powerful combination."

"So, what did you do?" I am riveted by her speech and can't wait to hear as she grins and laughs softly. "I made it my mission to stand out, like he did. I wrote him little notes that I posted through a gap in his locker, written on pink paper that I sprayed with perfume. One letter every day for two weeks until he worked out who sent them."

"What did they say?" I am so interested I'm hanging onto her every word and she giggles. "I listed every reason why he should go out with me and signed them 'mystery girl.' There was a new reason for every day."

"Like what?"

"Oh, you know the sort of thing. I'm good fun, loyal and hard working. Boring stuff really, until I decided to mix it up a little. My notes got cheekier and more elaborate as I imagined our life together. I told him where we would go, what we would do, and painted a picture of an exciting future. It became a delicious game that I loved playing. I used to wait for him to go to class and post my notes. I got in loads of trouble with my teachers for being late to class, but I didn't care. I wanted Elvis Carlton and I was going to get him."

"So, what happened, did he find out, catch you in the act?"

Pauline laughs softly and the look in her eye tells me she's right back there in the past as she remembers the sweetest memory.

"I was at my locker one day gathering my books and felt someone behind me. Before I could turn around, he leaned down and sniffed my neck and said, "Gotcha mystery girl." Let me tell you Poll, my heart was banging out of control and I can still hear him whisper, 'I know it's you and now you've got to honour every promise you made me, starting after school.' Well, let me tell you, I was so excited I thought I'd burst. The other girls were listening in and I felt so powerful. It had worked. I'd reeled him in and now I had to keep him there. Well, we met up after school and we've been together ever since. So, you see, Polly, if you want something badly enough, you just have to work out the way there."

"How did he know it was you? Did someone see you posting the letters?"

Pauline winks. "Bloody perfume gave it away. I used to spray my Channel number 5 on it. I used to work in Superdrug and in those days, we were allowed to have the nearly empty sample bottles. I always grabbed the Channel number 5 because it was what Marilyn Monroe went to bed in every night. You see Polly, I want the best I can get and that perfume and Elvis Carlton were the best in my eyes and that's never changed."

I grin as I think about Pauline and her 'Channel number five.' The fact she says it wrong makes me love her more, there's absolutely nothing not to like about Pauline Carlton and I could listen to her stories all day long.

She looks at me with a determined expression and says firmly, "You see, Poll, I never looked back. I made it my business to get what I wanted, and I looked for a way to get it. Sometimes you need to make a bold statement to get ahead, and it's the positioning that counts. Take my kids, for instance. I knew the power of a name and nothing will change my mind on that. Elvis has always stood out because of his and I have always blended into the shadows with mine. Successful women aren't called Pauline, so when I had my family, I had that in mind. Miles sounds posh and intelligent, and the fact we could afford to send him to a private school set him up for a good job later in life. His name and history assured him of that. Jessica and Freddie are the same, and they wouldn't be in their positions now if they were called Jason or Sharon. If they were, it would be because they were exceptional at what they do. You see, a name can open doors in the first place but it's up to the individual to prove their worth, so what I'm trying to say, babe, is if you are unhappy with your job, decide what you want and set about getting it, either the unusual way like me, or just by finding what you need to succeed."

The door creaks open, interrupting our conversation, and Miles pops his head around it. "I'm sorry mum but dad says hurry up he's starving and unless some food joins the alcohol in his system, he won't be able to honour that promise he made you last night."

Catching the slight disgust on Miles's face, I giggle as Pauline jumps up quickly. "Bloody man will say anything to get me to feed him. Come on, Poll, lecture over, let's go and grab some roast beef, I'm a dab hand at a Yorkshire pudding too."

As I follow her out, her words accompany me. Pauline is an inspirational woman and I am digesting every word she said. Can I really change my future so easily? I owe it to myself to at least try.

CHAPTER 17

I feel a little deflated as we head back from a lovely time spent with Elvis and Pauline.

It gave me an insight into how a proper family operates, and I liked it so much I could have moved in and become an adopted member of their family.

They are so much fun to be around, and I can't remember the last time I laughed so much.

Miles was attentive and sweet and even I started to believe we were boyfriend and girlfriend, which makes it even more difficult to reason with myself. This is all wrong and yet so right at the same time. I'm liking the turn my life has taken, but it's all built on a lie and I'm increasingly becoming uncomfortable about that.

I must fall silent because as we sit in the car outside the village hall, my designated drop off point, Miles says softly, "What are you thinking?"

"I'm not sure really, but I know I've loved today. Your parents are amazing and such good company it's made me think a little on my own life."

"Then stop."

"What?"

"Thinking, it will only get you into trouble."

"Are you serious?"

"Yes. You are feeling bad about deceiving my parents because you like them. I feel bad about it because I love them, which is why it has to be this way."

He sighs and turns to face me, and the sadness in his eyes causes my heart to sink. "Mum and dad are only happy because they think I'm happy. They haven't been since Kate did the dirty on us and for the first time since it happened, it's almost like old times. Don't underestimate how much that means because this is the best Christmas present we could have given them."

"But what happens when it's over, do we tell them we split up or something, won't that upset them?"

He shakes his head. "No, because it will show them that I've moved on and am capable of dating again and finding someone better than Kate, although that won't be hard because in mum's eyes, everyone's better than Kate."

He throws me a wry smile but my heart sinks even further because he's reminding me this is just temporary, a cunning plan to make everything better with his family and while I still feel bad about it, I understand why he's doing it. I'm not sure what damage it's doing to my heart though because the more time I spend with Miles Carlton, the more I like him and as sure as Christmas is coming, my feelings will be the ruin of me.

However, I'm here now, so I paste a bright smile on my face and say, "Well, if you know what you're doing, that's ok but if they find out, it was all your idea and I tried to talk you out of it, ok."

"Ok."

He smiles and I stare at him, mesmerised, as his eyes

twinkle with mischief and something else. It feels a little awkward, so I say loudly, "Anyway, I should be going."

"This doesn't feel right."

His words stop me from wrenching the door open and I say, "What doesn't?"

"Dropping you off here. What if someone attacks you on the way home? I would be responsible."

I'm not sure what to say because I'm not looking forward to walking the dark streets on my own and now I've met his parents twice, it does seem a little mistrusting. So, making an instant decision, I say, "Ok, thanks."

"Really, you trust me to know where you live?"

"Why, shouldn't I?"

He grins. "No, I'm happy because it means you're relaxing a bit around me and I'm glad about that."

"That's good because I don't live alone as you know and have a ninja neighbour downstairs who is licenced to kill."

"I expected as much, after all, I would expect nothing less from a Bond girl."

I direct him to the flat and it feels nice, more like a proper date, although I have to keep on reminding myself it's anything but.

By the time we reach my street and pull into the visitor's parking space, I'm hating the thought of him going at all.

Part of me wished it *was* a proper date and we were a proper couple. This may be a business arrangement, but it's becoming more than that for me. I really like Miles and if I could go and pluck a boyfriend off the shelf in 'Boyfriends R Us' it would be him every time.

Realising he's waiting for me to leave, I say awkwardly, "Um, thanks, I enjoyed myself and I appreciate the lift home."

Before I embarrass myself, I make to leave and a hesitant voice stops me, "Um, Polly…"

I think I hold my breath, "Yes?"

A hand on my arm pulls me around to face him and I swear I can see my heart beating against my skin through my clothes and winter coat. "I've enjoyed this, um, the time we've spent together, I don't suppose..."

Oh, please kiss me, dear God, I'll be a good girl forever if you give me that at least.

"You would meet me on Thursday."

"Why?"

Imagining some sort of weird party he's arranged where I have to dress up as a Christmas tree or something, I realise that wouldn't matter as long as I was with him.

"It's late night shopping and I really need to get my family some presents. I'm rubbish at choosing, so would you help, I'll buy you dinner to say thank you?"

"Ok," Wow, not even a hesitation, what a loser. Why can I never play things cool? I couldn't agree fast enough, and I am mentally kicking myself for being so easy.

He sighs with what I think is relief and I expect it's because like most men, he can now pass on the responsibility of thinking of something his family will actually want for Christmas, although I'm not really sure I'm up to that.

His hand is still on my arm and I wish the whole of me would join it. Thinking of those arms wrapped around me is an image that will keep me warm tonight. Instead I will have to grab my latest romance to make me feel better because that's all I can do these days, live my life through the pages of a book.

"Anyway, maybe I should go."

The air is thick with tension and there's a slight edge to his voice, so I say quickly, "Of course, you must be tired."

"Not really, are you?"

"Not really."

The shadows from the night sky provide us a place to hide as the hint of something magical lingers in the air. It's cold outside, freezing in fact, but inside this car it's as warm as a summer's day. Miles can't appear to form words and that has always been a problem for me, so we just stare stupidly at each other, waiting for something neither of us are prepared for.

A sharp knock on the window causes me to jump out of my skin and I look out with surprise to see Jonathan from downstairs, stamping his feet and blowing on his hands. "I thought that was you, Polly."

Quickly, I wind my window down, feeling so angry I almost can't speak because he has interrupted the moment when my life was at a crossroads.

"Thank God, I thought it was you, I don't suppose you've got my spare key. I've locked myself out and I'm freezing to death out here."

He looks past me to Miles and the look in his eyes makes me want to laugh out loud. "Who's your friend?"

He smiles at Miles with a 'come and get it' look and I stifle a giggle as Miles smiles awkwardly. "Um, Miles, I'm pleased to meet you."

"Holy Christmas fairy, where did you find him, Polly because forget the key, I'm heading there right now?"

I start to laugh as Miles looks at me with astonishment as Jonathan openly stares at him in adoration.

The icy blast of air that enters the car causes me to act and I say quickly before I lose my nerve, "Come on, I'll make us some coffee to warm up, fancy some, Miles?"

Jonathan fans himself and throws me a, 'I can't believe you just said that' look and Miles apparently can't get out of the car quickly enough as he says, "Great, thanks."

Feeling as if the night is not over yet, we all head inside and feel the warmth greet us as we step in from the cold and slam the door on a night that is sure to end up a white paradise in the morning.

CHAPTER 18

e pile inside the flat and as I throw my keys on the table, I say to Jonathan. "I wonder where Suze is?"

He shrugs and looks a little furtive, which sets my alarm bells ringing almost immediately. They are good friends, probably better than me and Suze. I know she told him, it's written all over his face, and by the look on his, I'm not going to like it.

Now we're here, it reminds me that I have a man in my flat for the first time since Richie and it feels a little strange. Jonathan is always here, so he doesn't count and as usual makes himself at home on the couch and groans. "You're a lifesaver Polly, I could have died from the cold tonight."

Unwrapping myself from my layers, I smile at Miles and say quickly, "Let me take your coat. Make yourself comfortable and I'll fix you a coffee."

He quickly shrugs out of his coat and Jonathan pats the seat beside him. "You can sit here and tell me all Polly's secrets. If you don't know any, I'll fill in the gaps."

He winks and Miles laughs and I leave them chatting like old friends as I head into our small kitchen to make coffee.

Now I'm alone, I have time to process my thoughts. Something was going to happen in that car, I just know it. Jonathan interrupted a moment in time that may have changed everything. Then again, he may have saved me from something that could have made me look desperate and a fool. I wonder what Miles was about to say because it was obvious he had something on his mind and as the kettle starts boiling, I wonder what it was. Will I ever find out?

I hear the low murmur of voices coming from the other room and the gentle laughter of two people who are obviously laughing about me. I know Jonathan and he's got a wicked tongue. None of my secrets are safe in there, but I'm surprised to find I don't care. I want Miles to know everything about me, and I want to know everything about him. He's the first man I feel immediately comfortable with and it's almost as if we know what each other likes and dislikes - soulmates?

As Elvis would say, I bloody well hope so.

Grabbing what's left of the biscuit packet, I head back into the room balancing a tray laden with something hot to warm us up inside and Jonathan groans his appreciation. "Polly, you're an angel. In fact, I was just telling Miles about the time we all went dressed as fairies to the local pub on Christmas Eve. Do you remember, we all wanted the pink outfit but it would only fit Suze? We were spitting jealously that night because she pulled that man with the Porsche on the strength of it, you know, the stockbroker from Hackney who turned out to be a pervert."

Miles looks surprised and I say quickly, "I'm trying to forget that night, Jonathan and the subsequent police enquiry we got involved in."

"Police enquiry? That sounds serious."

Jonathan nods. "Yes, we were contacted by a police officer the next morning. Apparently, they wanted us to give a statement because Tony, whatever his name was, got arrested on the way home by a hit squad. He'd been under surveillance for months and turned out to be the Hackney Horror who preyed on women in his regenerated flat. He used to drug their drinks and take them home with him for a night of passion, and they woke up the next morning with no recollection of how they got there. It was only because Polly was so clumsy that Suze didn't receive the same treatment."

"Clumsy, surely not." Miles stifles a grin as I nod.

"I knocked her drink over with my oversized wings and jabbed my wand in his eye. I was trying to spin on the spot like one of those ballerinas in the music boxes, and it went wrong. He left in an ambulance but went home in a police car; not a happy Christmas for him that year."

"Or this one, I'm sure. Didn't he get five years hard labour as a result of the trial? I quite fancied the judge by the way."

Miles is looking between us in total astonishment which makes me giggle and then Jonathan does the decent thing and says loudly, "Where are my keys, darling? I need my beauty sleep, its hell being an elf at Christmas."

"An elf."

Miles looks surprised and I grin. "Jonathan's an elf at Barrington's Garden centre. He went for the job as Santa but wasn't fat enough."

"Correction, darling, I went for the job as the Christmas fairy but wasn't feminine enough."

Turning to Miles, he smiles in his lopsided way and says enthusiastically, "Get Polly to bring you in. I'll reserve you a spot on Santa's knee and if he refuses, you can sit on my..."

"Bye Jonathan."

Handing him the keys, I roll my eyes and he laughs loudly. "I can take a hint, darling. Night, night and don't do anything I wouldn't do. Lovely meeting you, Miles, I hope it won't be the last time, next time we'll do lunch."

He winks and then heads off, leaving blissful silence behind. Jonathan is a force of nature that has to be experienced to believe and Miles grins, "You have a nice neighbour, I'm glad."

"Yes, I do."

I take a sip of my coffee and look at him from under my lashes. It doesn't seem strange him being here. He looks perfectly at home and the fact I have a man in my flat, and nobody is home, should make me worried but it doesn't – it just feels right.

To my surprise, Miles sets his mug down and says gently, "Um, Polly…"

He seems unsure and I feel my hands trembling as I try to look normal, while inside I'm shaking with something alien to me. Nerves, need, anticipation, all rolled up into a big ball of hope.

"Yes."

"I've really enjoyed your company, it's been fun."

Oh no, is he breaking up with me already? Has he had second thoughts about this arrangement and decided I was right and this is wrong?

I almost don't want to hear it and say nervously, "What is it, Miles?"

"I was just thinking, well, it was something my mum said when you went to the loo."

My heart is pounding. Maybe she told him to ditch me as I was obviously a complete mess with no direction in my life and I almost don't want to hear it.

"Would you like to come to Christmas dinner with us?"

He looks at me with a hopeful expression and I stare back at him in shock. "Christmas dinner?"

He nods, looking excited. "Mum told me to invite you but

I wasn't sure if you had plans. I did tell her you probably have, but she told me to ask you, anyway. I know you may feel a little uncomfortable about it but we would love to have you, if you want to come, of course."

Picturing my planned Christmas of pyjamas and a tub of Quality Street perched on the exact spot he is sitting now, it's not a difficult decision to make. Imagining the sort of Christmas Miles and his family has makes my mouth water at the thought of experiencing a Christmas I would normally only ever see on the television. However, there's a part of me that thinks I should refuse, it's not right, a step too far with the deception and so against my wishes, I say sadly, "I don't think I can."

I'm not sure if it's my imagination or not, but his face falls and he whispers, "I see."

"You see what?"

"You're uncomfortable with it. I know I shouldn't ask, after all, we've only known each other a couple of days really but well, I thought…"

"What?"

My heart jumps around inside me as I pray for him to declare his undying love for me, but he just smiles and says brightly, "It's fine. We're still on for Thursday, aren't we? I could pick you up from work if you like."

My mood instantly lifts as I picture the moment when Miles steps out of his shiny sports car in full view of the workers and runs towards me with his arms outstretched. I would fall into them and he would spin me around in front of Richie and Gail and we would share a deep passionate kiss like in the movies, before driving off and covering them with a puff of exhaust fumes.

"I finish at five."

He looks a little relieved and says brightly, "Great, I'll

look forward to it. I hope your shopping skills are brushed up and primed because I have a lot of decisions to make."

"I won't let you down, I'll draw up a list of ideas and work out a plan so that we can work methodically through the stores to maximise the time we have."

Miles looks a little shocked and I stifle a grin. Maybe I've just let it slip that I'm seriously weird when it comes to lists and planning. He won't know but I can feel a spreadsheet coming on already at the delicious thought of planning his Christmas shopping and I say quickly, "Do you have a budget in mind, I could start with that?"

"A budget?"

He looks slightly worried and I say with determination. "I need to know what I'm playing with. How many presents do you need and what's your budget for each one? Maybe you could text me the details along with their hobbies, likes and dislikes and what you bought them last year. It would be helpful if you could also send a list of their favourite shops and what you were thinking of buying them. We could go for gift vouchers but it's way more fun unwrapping an actual present, don't you think? Much more thoughtful, really. Obviously, we would need gift-wrap and it would be handy if the stores offered a free service..."

"Polly." I look up into his rather amused face that has somehow crossed the room and is standing right before me, inches from my own. I almost take a step back in shock as his fingers brush against my lips and he says softly, "Hush."

His eyes twinkle as he stares into mine and whispers, "No lists, no plans and no budgets. We will just head out and see what happens. I want us to have fun and enjoy a leisurely evening with none of the stress that Christmas can bring."

His mouth hovers inches from mine and I lean a little closer. In my mind I am willing our lips to touch, but he pulls back and says firmly, "I should be going. I have a breakfast meeting and need to go over my notes."

I watch with disappointment as he grabs his coat and says brightly, "Thanks for the coffee, and for agreeing to help on Thursday, you're a lifesaver."

"No problem."

My heart sinks as he heads towards the door and the moment of magic goes with him. Remembering my manners, I walk with him and hate the fact I wish he would stay. I'm almost tempted to do something rash like launch myself on him and beg him not to go, and in my mind, I do, but instead I say softly, "Thanks for a lovely day, Miles. Your family is amazing."

What I really mean is *he* is amazing but I won't be that desperate woman which is how I feel right now.

He turns to me and smiles. "Sleep well, Polly. I'll look forward to catching up on Thursday."

The door closes softly behind him and I fight the wave of disappointment that brings. Maybe I should make up an excuse not to take this any further because it could cost me my heart when Christmas is over and he leaves for London. I will be left behind in Slip End, remembering a time when my life was magical and I almost had it all.

CHAPTER 19

"*H*i Polly, how was your weekend?"

Cindy smiles sweetly as I take my place in line early on Monday morning.

"Great thanks, I spent it with Miles."

Gail snorts beside me and says quickly, "Anyway, Cindy, did I tell you that Richie made me dinner on Saturday night, it was so romantic. In fact, *he's* so romantic and I can't believe how lucky I am to have such an amazing man in my life. You know, he's always surprising me with little gifts and treats, I'm such a lucky girl."

"Bloody trains, there should be a law against them."

Marion interrupts the conversation – luckily and Gail shakes her head disapprovingly. "I hope you signed the late register Marion; it won't have gone unnoticed that you're late. I would be careful if I were you, we're all hanging by a thread here."

"Shut up, Gail, nobody's interested in what you have to say."

There's an awkward silence as Marion tells it how it is, and I know she's unhappy about something because she's not normally so abrupt. Gail huffs, "How rude, apologise at once because if Richie thinks you're bullying me…"

"I said shut it, Gail, you know, maybe Richie isn't being completely honest with you. God knows he does have previous for dishonesty."

"Excuse me?"

Gail's voice is tight and her eyes angry, and Cindy looks at me with astonishment. There's a terrible atmosphere here today and I say softly, "What is it, Marion?"

She grabs a nearby cracker and stuffs it unceremoniously before lowering her voice, "I heard a conversation when I arrived that I almost wished I hadn't."

She lowers her voice and I have to strain to hear her above the noise of the conveyor belt. "I overheard Mr Sullivan talking to that woman he's recruited. They were on the staircase above me near the staff room and I heard him say Sparkle Crackers may not make it to next Christmas if sales don't pick up."

"Oh no, do you think…"

Cindy looks upset as Marion nods. "This could be Sparkle Cracker's last Christmas."

"But what would we do for money?"

Cindy looks as if she's about to cry as Richie heads across looking agitated. "Get a move on ladies, no time for gossiping. Just to inform you there will be an announcement during morning coffee. Mr Sullivan will be addressing the workers, so make sure you're not loitering in the toilets, or outside for a ciggie."

"What's happening, Richie, is everything ok?"

Gail looks worried and for a second his face relaxes as he looks at her, causing another dagger to stab my heart. He never looked at me like that, in fact, nobody has ever looked at me like that. Suddenly, it hits me that I'm no longer concerned about the two people beside me. They can have each other as far as I'm concerned because as much as it pains me to admit it, they do make a lovely couple. It's just that, well, I would love to be someone's world like Gail is obviously his. Will I ever experience that feeling? I wish I could, with Miles actually, and I am still holding onto that last shred of hope that something magical will happen this Christmas and all my dreams will come true.

Richie snaps, "Can I have a word please, Gail?"

She quickly drops her cracker and follows him out and Marion snaps, "Typical. Probably gone off for a quick pick me up before the bad news hits, disgusting."

We carry on stuffing our crackers with an air of depression settling around us. This doesn't look good – at all. We carry on with our work quietly, without the usual buzz of conversation that gets us through a depressing shift and I imagine the impending announcement is weighing heavily on everyone's mind as we struggle to understand what closure would mean for us. I wonder what I would do for money. Would I be forced into escortdom by my desperation? Can I look forward to many nights spent with ageing businessmen as I accompany them around town? What happens when my looks fade and my clientele dry up? The future is bleak and the picture in my mind is not the one I thought it would be, so it's with a heavy heart that I put down my cracker and head to the canteen for the impending announcement.

Grabbing a seat next to Marion and Cindy, I note that Gail is huddled in the corner with Richie, their heads together, keeping the whole world out. The buzz of conversation all around us stills as Mr Sullivan and his glamourous assistant march into the room and take their place at the front, with several anxious eyes all pointing in their direction.

You could hear a pin drop as Mr Sullivan clears his throat and looks at us with a serious expression.

"Thanks for coming, I'll keep this short."

Marion nudges me and I throw her a brave smile. Maybe it's not as bad as she thinks it is.

"Anyway, I'm sure you've heard the rumours that things have been difficult for quite some time. Our more senior staff will know that we are nowhere near as busy as we used to be, reflected in the dwindling workforce and lack of orders."

He clears his throat and says sadly, "The world is changing and we are struggling to keep up. More competition and cheaper alternatives are increasingly making this an industry that's falling on its knees. Miss Constable was brought in to try and generate some interest for our product, but she's climbing a steep mountain. We may not have the time she needs to turn this around, so I wanted to give you the heads up. I may not be able to keep this place going another year unless business picks up. Obviously, we will try and do the best we can, but I thought you should know. The new year will be make or break for us and the first quarter will seal our fate. Unless the orders increase, we will have no other choice but to call it a day and wrap things up. I just wanted to prepare you for that, although I hope I stand here in April with a smile on my face and a tale of how things came good in the end. I'm a realist though and know this may be the last year a Sparkle Cracker takes pride of place on a Christmas table. I'm sorry to be the bearer of such sad news, but I want you to know the truth rather than hear the rumours that have been circulating for some time."

He smiles bravely. "Anyway, we're not beaten yet, so everyone pray for a miracle, we're going to need one that's for sure."

He nods to his companion who throws us all a sympathetic look as they vacate the room and Cindy says with a tremor to her voice, "What will we do if Sparkle Crackers goes pop?"

Marion shrugs, "Something will come up. Either a new job, or a miracle. I know there's a new retail development opening in the spring next year near the railway station. Maybe we could apply for jobs there."

"Maybe." I look at my companions and say sadly, "It won't be the same though, will it?"

For a moment we sit and remember when we were just happy to moan about how much we hated our job, now it seems unbearable that we could lose it. It's funny how attached we get to routine and the mundane. Maybe this is the slap in the face I needed to pick myself up and do something with my life. Perhaps this is the nudge I require making me look outside my comfort zone and move onto pastures new. I have until April, at least. Perhaps I should look for a job in London as Miles seems to love it there so much, but I don't want to. I want to have the luxury of being secure in my job while an opportunity makes it way to me. I want Sparkle Crackers to survive because it deserves its place at the nation's Christmas tables. Not some mass-produced creation from China. No, this is a British company that deserves to be saved. But how on earth is that ever going to happen in today's climate? As I said before, the product is the same as it has been for the last twenty years. Who wants that in today's world? It's all about innovation and the new and unknown. Who wants the same joke year in year out and how many plastic magnifiers can a person cope with?

As we make our way back to work with doleful expressions, I think of Pauline and her amazing crackers and my heart sinks. Yes, people want more, they *expect* more, and our business is doomed if we think we have any hope in competing with that.

CHAPTER 20

*T*here's something wrong with Susie. She looks the same, talks the same and walks the same, but her mind is definitely elsewhere.

We are slumped on the sofa watching the Christmas channel and usually she would be providing a running commentary about what will happen, ruining the magic and making me laugh with anecdotes and her hilarious way of picking up on every fault in the characters and story. Not today. Today she just stares at the screen, but I'm not sure she's even seeing it.

"Is everything ok, Suze?"

"I'm sorry."

She shakes her head and looks at me as if she's just remembered I'm here.

"You don't seem yourself, in fact, I'm betting you can't remember a thing about this storyline."

Her eyes flick to the television and then back to me, and I can tell something is definitely weighing heavily on her mind.

"You remember, Kevin."

My heart sinks, please not him.

"Yesss…" I draw out the syllable as if I'm in no hurry to hear the reply, and she sighs heavily.

"I think I've just messed his life up."

"What are you talking about?"

"Well, I was doing what I intended to do and just carrying on. I tried to put him to the back of my mind and kick him firmly into touch. The thing is, I was out with a client the other day. You know that party I told you about at the Hoo."

I nod and she sighs. "Anyway, I was escorting a rather lovely chap as it happened. He was good looking, funny, and kept me in stitches all night. His name was Edward, Eddie for short, and was the perfect pick me up that I needed."

"That sounds promising." I smile, happy to hear that she had a good time, but she sighs.

"I thought so too. Anyway, we started chatting and got onto the subject of past customers. He was interested and such a good listener, so I told him about Kevin. Well, to cut a long story short, by the end of it he asked me if it was Kevin Potter by any chance. Well, I'm sure you are as surprised as me, I mean, what are the odds of him knowing him but the shock on my face must have told him what he needed to know because he just laughed and shook his head. He told me he knew him. In fact, Kevin had recommended the agency and told him the girls were sure things and if he was at a loose end, he should have a little fun."

"I'm sorry, Suze." My heart sinks at the pain in her eyes and she wipes a lone tear away furiously. "Luckily, Eddie was a gentleman. He was so sweet and told me he was never looking for a good time in the same way as Kevin meant it and just wanted some female company to a function he would have sold his granny to keep from attending. Anyway, we pushed it aside and carried on with our evening, but it played on my mind and I suppose a little of the sparkle left me. At the end of the night he asked me if I fancied a nightcap."

"Oh no, you didn't..."

Susie looks up and her small smile makes my heart settle, "Oh no, nothing like that. Well, we sat in a room where they were serving nightcaps and he told me he knew Kevin quite well as it happens *and* his wife. He was staring at me so intently I thought I was in trouble and must have looked terrified because he took hold of my hand and said really sweetly that I wasn't to be worried. He was actually Kevin's boss and knew all about Kevin and his wandering eye. He also knew his wife Joanne and was disgusted by the tales he had heard because he knew they were expecting their first baby. Apparently, Kevin has quite the reputation and doesn't just proposition escorts. Eddie's had some customer complaints from women who have come across Kevin, and he's had enough. He asked if I would tell him everything and he would prepare a case against him."

She looks at me in complete horror and I smile reassuringly. "That's a good thing, isn't it? He sounds like a total sleaze and if anything, you will be doing the women of the world a favour."

"Not his wife, though."

"Especially his wife, poor woman, who wants to be saddled with a creep like that for a husband?"

"But the baby, it's not fair to put stress on a pregnant woman. What if they split up and he loses his job? How will they pay for the baby, they need lots of security you know, and it will be all my fault? A family will be torn apart and I'm not sure if I can live with that on my conscience."

Flicking the television off, I jump into the seat beside her and place my arm around her shoulders. "This isn't your fault, it's his. You've done nothing wrong and circumstances have dictated what happens in his life. He was the one who ruined things, not you. You didn't know he was married, he conveniently kept that from you."

"Yes, but I went against every rule in my book. I slept with a customer, that makes me a…"

"No, it doesn't." I stare at her with the firmest look I have ever given. "You fell in love. You weren't paid to do that and it's not your fault he turned out, not so Prince Charming. If I were you, I would put it to the back of your mind and concentrate on what makes you happy. He has made this bed and it's up to him to iron out the creases. His boss sounds nice though, maybe he can restore your faith a little in men."

She nods and a small smile graces her lips. "He was nice, actually. The perfect gentleman who asked if I wouldn't mind meeting him later this week to discuss this over dinner. Not as a paying customer, just as a…"

"Date?" I look at her hopefully and she rolls her eyes and laughs softly. "A business meeting. Honestly, Polly, you look for the romance in everything. Anyway, speaking of which, how are things going with your own business deal?"

My face must fall because she looks concerned. "Hey, what's happened?"

"Nothing."

"Then why the face?"

"I can't help my face, Suze, it's the only one I've got."

"Then why are you looking so upset? I thought things were going well."

"They are, I suppose, it's just that everything's going wrong all at once."

"Tell me, I could use the distraction because hearing about somebody else's troubles will make mine look better."

"Well, firstly, I may not have a job next year if Sparkle Crackers doesn't up its game and actually sell some."

She looks horrified and I nod, "Sad but true. Also, I have fallen in love with Miles's family, you remember, they invited me for Sunday lunch. Well, they are seriously nice and such good company and now they've asked me for Christmas and I've had to turn the invitation down but I would love to go really, but I can't."

"Why not?"

"Because this friendship is built on a lie. Miles is playing a cruel trick on them, making them believe he's happy and it feels wrong to be part of that, also…"

A light sparks in her eye as she says softly, "You like him."

I nod miserably. "Again, sad but true. What am I going to do, Suze? I may lose my job and the nicest people I have ever met in my life, present company aside."

We share a smile and she returns the favour and slings her arm around my shoulder, pulling me hard against her. "Don't overthink this, Polly. Just enjoy the moment because as moments go, it's one that doesn't come along too often. Regarding the job, something will come up, it always does and if you lose it, it's because a better one is around the corner and it was always meant to be. As for Miles, well, that's a tricky one because you don't have long."

"Long for what?"

"To make him fall in love with you, if you want to, that is."

"Make him fall in love with me, how exactly?"

She screws up her face and looks thoughtful. "I'm guessing just be yourself. I mean, who wouldn't fall in love with you? If he doesn't, he's not worth bothering with, anyway."

She reaches across and flicks the remote. "Let's see how it's done, shall we. Maybe Claudia and James can show us, after all, this is a movie and a Christmas one at that. There's always a happy ending at Christmas, it's a well known fact."

As the film resumes playing, we settle back in our seats and try to get our heads back in the story. However, I can't concentrate because all our problems are swirling around my mind and just won't go away. I think we both need a Christmas miracle this year, and I wish I knew where to find one.

$\mathcal{A}$s it happens miracles come when you least expect them and an opportunity presents itself the very next day.

As usual, I am back on the production line and after a while decide to grab a comfort break. This is usually frowned upon outside of our breaks but it's cold in here today and I did have a large latte on the way in this morning instead of my usual regular one, which has made me more desperate than usual.

I think I'm alone in the toilets and merrily going about my business when I hear a soft voice speaking outside my cubicle. At first, I pay no attention and then shamelessly listen in when I hear what she's talking about.

"I won't change my mind, mum, the writing's on the wall in this place and I don't think anything will change. I'm getting zero interest and that job at Remington's is a godsend because if I'm not mistaken, I won't have one here next year, anyway."

There's a short pause and then she laughs lightly, "Way more money. In fact, it's a dream come true. I've always wanted to work in Scotland and this is my perfect opportunity. Gavin is living there and I could bunk in with him."

Again, a small pause and she laughs. "Who knows, this time he may make an honest woman of me. No, this is the right decision. I'll hand in my letter of resignation tomorrow and accept the job. New year, new start, new path to tread. Anyway, how are you, is dad still working on his golf handicap?"

The door bangs as she leaves the room, and I sit for a moment in shock. That can only have been one person, and I can't believe what I just heard. Miss Constable is jumping from the sinking ship. Poor Mr Sullivan.

As I wash my hands, I think about what I've heard. Miss Constable is leaving, she doesn't think Sparkle Crackers will make it and she should know, she is the expert, after all. My worst fears have been confirmed and there will be no Christmas miracle inside one of our crackers. Somehow, the last few days and everything that's happened all merge into one huge problem and comes back to bite me. Miles, his family, Suze and Kevin, somehow get tangled up together and at its heart is Sparkle Crackers. So many problems and so little time.

Then it hits me. An idea emerges from the maelstrom and plants itself firmly in my mind. This is it, my turning point in life. My big break – possibly both in business and pleasure. If I can pull this off, it will define my future, fingers crossed anyway. Am I brave enough to try, or just plain stupid?

"Hurry up Polly, Richie's asking where you are, don't give him any more reasons to hand you that written warning."

Marion pokes her head around the door and I snap back to reality. "Sorry, on my way."

I quickly join her and head back to work, an idea taking root in my mind. Now I need to be brave enough to act on it.

∾

IF MY MORNING WAS BAD, it gets even worse in the afternoon.

Gail has decided to talk nonstop about Richie, and it's seriously getting on my nerves. "You see, guys, my parents love Richie. My mum only said the other day how perfect we are together. In fact, Richie told me he had never fallen in love before because what we have is better than anything he's ever had and now he knows he was just passing time until he met me."

She looks across at me slyly and then says brightly, "Oh, I'm sorry Polly, I keep on forgetting you dated once. I hope I haven't upset you."

The silence speaks a thousand words as my co workers wait for the storm to hit, but I just rise above it and shrug. "He did me a favour, actually."

Gail rolls her eyes. "Of course, he did."

"I'm not lying, Gail because quite frankly you're right. What I had with Richie wasn't love, it was just convenience. To be honest, I never really fancied him much, anyway. He was ok I guess, but nothing like Miles. I mean, there's a real man. Someone a girl would be proud to walk out with. Somebody who knows how to treat a girl right, not just expect her to indulge his love of quickies in the toilets. No, Miles is a gentleman and everything I thought I'd want in a man, not the child that Richie never seems to have grown up from. He was terribly boring; I mean, if you couldn't chat incessantly about goal averages and transfer windows, he wasn't interested. He only wanted to eat one meal, fish and chips, and wore the same pair of pants every day for a week. No, Gail, you're welcome to him because you did me a huge favour when you stole him from me because it left me free to find Miles."

I think Gail's about to explode when Cindy says with interest, "So, it's going well with Miles then."

"Oh yes, things couldn't be better." I plaster a dreamy look on my face and say casually, "He's picking me up tomorrow night after work to go Christmas shopping. It's late night at the mall and I expect we'll grab a table in Prezzo's afterwards. You know, the conversation never dries up and did I tell you about his family? Super successful and living in that posh street in Harpenden, you know, the one where the houses cost millions. Miles himself is very successful. He works in the city of London and has a really cool life there. Yes, I'm so lucky. So, thanks Gail. You did me a favour there."

Gail storms off, no doubt to report me to Richie for bullying, and the others laugh. Marion shakes her head, "She had that coming. I hope it wasn't just a story to wind her up because you deserve someone like him."

I feel a little bad but shake it off because even though I did tell the truth, I left a major part out - it's all pretence. The trouble is, *I'm* not pretending anymore and the thought of meeting up with Miles tomorrow is the only thing keeping me going. I wonder how I'll feel when Christmas is over and he returns home, leaving me to face possible redundancy and life on benefits because jobs are few and far between for a woman with no actual qualifications.

"May I have a word please, Polly?"

We look up and see Richie standing there looking so angry I can almost taste it. Gail is standing beside him, looking upset and sniffing as if to reinforce her misery. Resisting the urge to roll my eyes, I say pleasantly, "Of course."

"Follow me." Richie's voice is tight and angry as he snaps, "The rest of you, get back to work. Gail, you may go and take a moment, grab a cup of tea and take things easy."

I don't miss the smug look she shoots me and the angry

ones on the faces of my friends. Great, another hoop to jump through just to get through the day.

~

RICHIE DIRECTS me towards his office, which is actually just a cubby hole under the staircase with room for a desk and chair and not a lot more. I have to hover in the doorway because there isn't room for two people and as he lowers himself onto the wheelie chair, I prepare myself for the dressing down I am sure to receive.

He fixes me with a blank look and then says condescendingly, "You really must get over me, Polly. This constant sniping at Gail is just sad and you are letting yourself down."

I say nothing, which obviously makes him think he's hit the mark and he lowers his voice. "Listen, I know it's hard for you seeing me with another girl. I'm not a monster, I do know how difficult it must be. What we had was good at the time, but what I have with Gail is much better. You see, she is my soulmate, you were not. I know that must be difficult to hear, but sometimes a man must be cruel to be kind. Now, if I were you, I would try and forget about me. I know it must be hard, but you must. I'm not coming back to you as much as you may hope that will happen. Gail is trying to be brave listening to your bitchy comments all day, and it's a credit to her that she manages to continue with a smile on her face. So, count this as a verbal warning – off the record, of course, I do still care for my snuggle bunny after all."

He smiles as if he's being magnanimous and I can't believe what I'm hearing.

As he leans back in his chair and places his hands together almost as if he's praying, he fixes a patronising smile on his face as he says, "It will take time but you will get over me one day. I just want you to know that I'm here for you and if you ever need to talk, my door is always open. Now, let's say no more about it and carry on supporting each other through the crisis we are all facing. I'm afraid if I'm pushed, I may not be able to protect you from the first wave of redundancies, just putting that out there. So, before you return to work, do you have something you want to say to me, or Gail perhaps, maybe in the form of an apology."

He stares at me as if waiting, and I shrug.

"I do as it happens."

"Ok, say your piece and then you may go."

I shrug. "To be honest, Richie, I couldn't care less about you, Gail, or any of it. You see, I've moved on to bigger and better things and quite frankly, you did me a favour. If Gail's upset, I'm sorry but neither of you cared about my feelings while you rubbed your relationship in my face. However, that said, I wish you both well. I don't want to hold a grudge and if anything, I hope you'll both be happy and live happily ever after. So, if you don't mind, I'll leave you to get on with it because I no longer give a damn."

Turning on my heels, I walk away from his office feeling much better. I meant what I said, it no longer matters. They no longer matter and if anything, I wish them well. I just don't want them to pity me when there is no reason to. Gail is welcome to Richie; I had a lucky escape.

CHAPTER 22

*T*he journey home is a thoughtful one. The bus is crowded and the dampness in the air is not bothering me because I'm wrapped in my own thoughts. Can I do this? Will it work? I'm not so sure, and as I sit on the bus heading back to Slip End, what I'm planning to do seems a world away from something Polly Proudlock would do. Pauline Carlton, or Cotton on the other hand, wouldn't hesitate.

The more I think about her story, the more the idea takes shape. If Miss Constable is leaving, there will be a vacancy on the mezzanine level. I could do her job; I know I could. I would love to promote Sparkle Crackers and rescue it from the abyss. I would relish the chance to make a difference to so many lives and imagine the faces of the public and the joy they would receive as a result of my ideas.

Marion was right, it's time to shake this company up and bring it into the present. It's an outdated business model that no longer works, but if I'm to get Mr Sullivan's attention, I must be clever about it.

There was a reason I met Pauline and this is it. Her idea

has captured my imagination and if I'm to try and move myself from the production line, I need to be innovative, bold and adventurous.

I no longer see the crowds around me. The woman struggling to open a pushchair with one hand, while holding a screaming child in the other. I don't see the elderly woman blowing some warmth onto her hands as she shivers on the crowded bus with her plastic shopping bags at her feet. The music from the ear pods of the youth standing clutching the steel pole in front of me no longer irritates me. It all fades into the background as the excitement grips me of an opportunity to turn my life around along with those of my co workers.

Once I'm off the bus, I don't notice the steady drizzle that feels like sharpened knives against my face. The fact the wind is blowing no longer makes me grip my coat even tighter around my shivering body. The sound of a car passing with loud Christmas tunes blaring from the speakers doesn't distract me and the bright lights of the warm inviting houses I pass, no longer hold my inquisitive curiosity as I head home for the evening. Instead, I am buzzing with excitement inside. I am plotting and planning my way out of the ordinary and into an exciting new world - the management suite upstairs. I can almost picture my power suit and stockinged feet slipped into my stilettos as I celebrate another large order from a store that ceased trading with us years ago. I see the future as I walk in the present and it's a bright one, if only I can pull this off.

~

THE FLAT IS EMPTY as I head inside, it's obvious from the darkness and the eerie feeling of a place waiting for the spark of electricity to bring it to life again.

Shrugging off my coat, I am eager to begin a process that may backfire on me spectacularly and so, after making myself a mug of hot sweet tea, I settle down at my desk in the corner of the living room and extract a sheaf of pink paper that I use for correspondence from the drawer.

Then I take my posh pen that Suze bought me last Christmas and pen a letter that I hope changes my life.

Dear Mr Sullivan.

I hope you excuse my brutal honesty and boldness, but there is something you should know.

Your product is no longer fit for purpose.

I'm almost tempted to tear it up and start again, but really, I'm only stating the facts.

For over twenty years you have been selling the exact same product with the same tired ideas.
You need to change.
I am aware our sales are dwindling and I'm not surprised. I'm sorry to be so brutal, but you need to know.
The world is a very different one to when you started out all those years ago. It has moved on and tastes have changed. We have technology that shows us how wonderful life can be. Everything is possible and we all want more. Trends have changed and we are no longer content with the same things, year in year out.
Take your business, for example.
Put yourself in the place of your customer pulling one of your crackers every year. The same little gift inside, the magic fish that goes straight in the bin. The magnifying glass that gets caught up in the packaging. The joke that

everyone knows the punchline to and the paper hat that now seems cheap and slips down over your eyes before it tears in two and is no longer fit for purpose. It's hard to hear the groans and see the disgust on the faces of the person opposite who expected something better.

Now think about what those customers want when they sit down to pull one of your crackers. They want the thrill of what's inside. A special gift that will be useful, not landfill.

A joke or quote that makes them laugh and think. Something different to what's expected and something special that has meaning, not derision.

I can almost hear you saying now, 'We can't afford it.'

Well, let me tell you Mr Sullivan, sometimes the most valuable gifts we receive cost nothing.

I hope you don't mind me being so brutal, but it's something you need to hear. The next time I write will be with a list of suggestions that I think could save your business.

Yours good intentionally

A Friend.

Before I can think of changing one word, I slip the paper into an envelope and quickly address it. Then I take a stamp and grab my coat once more. This letter needs to make the last post before I change my mind. Mr Sullivan will hear me out, although he won't know it was me at all. Genius.

Quickly, I hurry downstairs and back onto the street before I can change my mind. It's not far to the post box on the corner, and if I'm lucky, it will land on his desk first thing in the morning. At worst, the next day, and yet I'm not even sure if I can wait that long. I want this to work for all the right reasons. I want to be better and I want to make a difference. This is that opportunity and if I fail it won't be because I didn't try at least.

ONCE THE LETTER is firmly on its way, I head home and feel a sense of satisfaction that isn't usually there. I did something. I did something bold and slightly foolish, and I like it.

Finally, Polly Proudlock is stepping outside her comfort zone and it feels good.

Now I've started, I can't stop and decide to seize the moment and grab my phone before I can change my mind.

I almost think she won't answer but then just before the answer phone kicks in, she says, "Polly, is everything alright?"

"Hi mum."

"What is it, are you sick, what about your job, is it boyfriend trouble?"

I take a deep breath because my mum is always like this. Keen to get the issues out in the open so she can deal with them quickly with minimal time taken from her day,

"No, everything's fine, I just thought I'd touch base, you know, check on you."

"Oh, I'm fine, darling, a little frazzled perhaps, I mean, it's difficult enough taking on another man's children as well as your own. Rebecca is Mary in the Nativity and has her own song and everything. Craig is turning out to be a talented footballer and requires a lot of ferrying around after school to various games etc, and Graham is working hard to pay for a fabulous Christmas. What about you, how's that boy you've been seeing, Simon, isn't it?"

I can hear shouting in the background and before I can

answer she shouts, "Ok, Aaron, make sure you've got your boots and a change of clothes."

She whispers, "We've got to go straight to Rebecca's rehearsal after the game, I can't keep up with them all. Then we have to collect Melanie from a friend's house and Aaron's game is in a different town completely to Craig's one. You know, it's hard being a mother to this bunch, but somehow I pull it off. Anyway, it's been lovely to chat but I must go, duty calls and all that."

I make to speak but then she says as an aside, "Oh, let me know if you're around for Christmas. If you come, you may have to sleep on the sofa, we've got Graham's parents for Christmas and they're taking the spare room. God knows I could use some help though; it's hard trying to be super woman. Anyway, love you. Have fun, bye…"

She cuts the call, leaving me feeling as worthless as a piece of Christmas wrapping paper discarded on the floor and then crushed into a ball and tossed in the wheelie bin. Then again, my mother has always made me feel like that. Something that was once exciting and special, but now no longer required. The bitter tears sting my eyes as I picture her giving her other children the sort of mum I always dreamed of. Why was she never that mum to me? Why was she always keen to move on to something else? My dad is no better, his phone always goes to voicemail and more often than not, he just leaves me a message when he knows I'll be working or in bed. Picturing Miles's parents, it burns even more because that is how I always imagined a family to be. Loving, happy and eager to spend time together.

Thinking of Pauline's invitation to Christmas dinner is a tempting offer I wish I could accept. Then again, how can I, it wouldn't be fair on any of us? It would only make me feel worse seeing something I will never be part of. Once again, I picture my Christmas, curled up on the settee in this flat, eating my way through a ready meal of Christmas Turkey and all the trimmings, while watching people on television showing me how I'm meant to be spending it.

The tears burn as I feel lonelier than I ever have before. It's hard being alone, especially at Christmas. Everyone else appears to have somewhere to go – except me. The world stops for one day and lets the magic in. Not mine. Families and friends come together to celebrate a magical event from the distant past that has so much influence and bearing on our lives today. Not me. I know I'm not alone, there are many other people in my position. In fact, I'm the lucky one because I do have somewhere to go. The fact I don't feel welcome doesn't really help, but mine is a self inflicted solitude, just so I don't feel the pain of rejection all over again when I see how different my mum is with her new family. Family number three to be precise and this time I hope it works out for her, for them, and possibly for me. One day she might wake up and realise she has another child, her own flesh and blood and one that needs her mum more than any of them. Until that time I'll have to make my own way in life and seize the opportunities it presents to me and maybe, just maybe, a Christmas miracle will happen.

CHAPTER 23

*T*hursday dawns and I head to work feeling a little worried. I wonder if Mr Sullivan has received my letter. In the cold light of day, I feel a little foolish. What was I thinking? It's almost hate mail, and he may get the police in to investigate the case of the poison pen letter.

My teeth chatter with more nerves than cold as I approach the factory staff entrance along with my dwindling band of fellow workers. As usual, the skies are grey and stormy and the only light on the horizon is the promise of seeing Miles again. It feels like forever since I saw him last and there's a stirring of excitement deep inside that's keeping me warm on this cold and frosty morning.

Harry the security guard nods as I pass and I wonder about him. He's always here, day in, day out and never speaks or smiles. Is he happy? Does he have a loving wife to go home to at night, presenting him with a warm home cooked meal and his slippers, along with a stiff glass of brandy to take the chill off? Is his house decorated beautifully with a tree and fairy lights and does he have children he actually enjoys spending time with? Then again, maybe his wife works opposite shifts just to make ends meet, so they can care for the children without having to pay out for childcare. Life is very different now to how it was in the past, money seems more important than quality family time.

The more I look around me, the more I picture people's lives. In every instance I imagine theirs are so much better than mine. Goodness, I need to get a grip because I am depressing myself and who wants to be depressed at the most wonderful time of the year? Certainly not the girl who is balancing on the precipice of excitement because I feel as if I am; something's about to change and I hope for the better.

I am first in today and as I pull on my overall and tuck my hair into the hairnet, I decide that whatever happens, I will change it up next year. Life's too short to merely exist. I want to live my best life and quite frankly this isn't it.

I see Mr Sullivan on the mezzanine level talking into his phone, looking weary and worried. I imagine he has bigger problems than mine that affect more than just himself, and I feel bad that I'm being selfish and wallowing in my own self-pity.

He must see me watching him because he turns his back and walks away and I wonder if he's had Miss Constable's resignation letter yet. Was it the first thing he saw when he ventured in this morning? I hope so, because it will pave the way for my own hostile takeover of a job that in reality should never be mine.

Marion soon joins me and mumbles, "God, I hate this place. I can think of so many other things I'd rather be doing right now."

"You'll miss it when it's gone, Marion."

For a moment we just share a look, both of us realising its better to moan about something we have, than something we've lost. If anything, it fuels my desire to save something that's as traditional as the Christmas Turkey.

Gail wanders in with Cindy who looks a little guilty to be seen talking to her and I feel bad. Today I feel bad for a lot of reasons and decide on the spot to do something that is long overdue - be the better person. So, I turn to Gail and smile brightly. She steps back a little as the full force of my smile hits her like a light sabre and looks a little worried as I say softly, "Gail, I um, think I owe you an apology for yesterday."

Everyone turns and looks at me in shock, probably thinking I suffered a blow to the head on the way in, and I smile at the group. "In fact, I want you all to know that I'm sorry for the 'atmosphere' that's been surrounding us since, well, Richie moved on with Gail."

Gail looks uncomfortable, probably anticipating the killer blow, but I just shake my head. "I'm sorry, Gail, because I took out my hurt and disappointment on you. I blamed you for taking Richie from me, instead of realising the problem lay with us. If it was right, it wouldn't have happened and I suppose he did me a favour. For the record, I think you make a lovely couple and if anything, I wish you both well. We shouldn't fight and bicker because we may not have long left. We must make what time we do have fun and something to look back on with fond memories. So, what do you say, shall we call a truce and put this messy business behind us?"

Wow, I feel amazing, like some kind of super woman who says and does the right thing for once. The admiring looks thrown my way from my two friends raises me to the level of a demi-goddess. Gail, to my surprise, has tears in her eyes and it's only now I realise that she has also been feeling the effects of all this, as she nods and says gratefully, "Oh thank you, Polly, it means a lot. I've hated the atmosphere and couldn't be myself. I really appreciate it, and for the record, I'm sorry too."

As the words leave her lips, the world rights itself. Gone is any animosity towards her, and in its place is a sense of calm. Maybe I didn't need to apologise, if anything I was the wronged woman in all of this, but what does that matter now? Hopefully, we can all move on and just make the most of the time we do have together.

As the whistle blows and the conveyor belt cranks into life, I think we all face the day with a lighter heart than we have for quite some time.

ALL DAY I've thought of little else than my ideas for the next letter I intend on writing to Mr Sullivan. It consumes my thoughts and I've kept my little secret locked in tightly as I go about my day. The atmosphere is lighter today despite the threat of redundancy looming over us, and for the first time in ages, I feel a ray of hope trying to wiggle through the darkness. In fact, the more I think of it, the more convinced I am that I can pull this off, so when 5 o'clock comes, I'm surprised to remember that Miles is picking me up. How on earth could I forget that?

Eagerly, I ditch my hated overalls and rip the safety goggles from my eyes as I struggle to make myself look presentable for somebody who will look like a fish out of water in the staff car park.

Marion is watching me with amusement and says with laughter, "I can't wait to meet this man for myself."

Cindy nods, "Me too, I bet he looks like Liam Hemsworth."

"I wish."

We all share a look because Liam Hemsworth is the subject of many conversations around the novelty line as we dream our way through a mundane day.

I see Gail and Richie in the corner sharing a cosy moment and smile. I feel nothing when I see them now, proving to me

I was right to draw a line under it all. It's the future that counts and I almost run out of the door, keen to see a man I am increasingly eager to spend time with.

My heart almost stops when, like a mirage, I see him waiting in the distance. Wearing a North Face padded jacket and Timberland boots, he leans against the door of his little red sports car, looking odd against his surroundings. He is the subject of many envious looks and Marion inhales sharply beside me, "Way to go, Polly, you weren't elaborating, in fact, if anything, you didn't do that man justice, way to go girl, I'm proud of you."

Cindy is equally impressed. "Bloody hell, Polly, why aren't you running by now. You are one lucky…"

I don't wait around to hear because I am suddenly power walking towards my future. The crowd parts as I head with determination to somebody who is ticking every box on my list because today is one of clarity and now I'm sure, I want Miles Carlton to be my actual boyfriend and I have until Christmas to make that happen.

CHAPTER 24

*M*iles grins as I dash across the courtyard towards him, conscious of several pairs of interested eyes on us. As I stop in front of him, I lean in and whisper, "Now it's your turn to play along. Don't look now, but my cheating ex and my replacement are in prime position to see that he has been replaced with a much better option.

Miles grins and leans closer, so to everyone watching it looks as if we are about to share an intimate moment and my heart flutters as if that really is the case.

He whispers, "Then let's add fuel to the fire, shall we?"

I almost pass out on the spot as he pulls my face towards his and leans down, his lips touching mine in a gentle pretence of a kiss. It would just take a slight movement on my part to lean in and seal the deal, but I appear to be frozen to the spot and it's not because of the weather.

Suddenly, putting on a show for Richie and Gail is no longer important, but connecting with Miles is. His eyes twinkle as he whispers, "Shall we?"

"What?"

My voice is breathy and disbelieving and he says huskily, "Put on a show."

"Ok"

My voice squeaks as I wait for the impossible dream, and as his lips touch mine, I no longer feel the cold. He tastes of cherry lip balm which for a moment throws me a bit, not even *I* wear lip balm, but all it does it fuel my need for something sweet, so I try not to just lick his lips to taste the product and give in to the moment of purest pleasure.

Miles Carlton kisses like he looks. Perfect. He wraps his padded arms around me and pulls me close and impressively devours my lips with a kiss so amazing I swear my toes curl. Not that I haven't imagined this moment a thousand times already, but nothing prepared me for how amazing it really is. I doubt even Liam Hemsworth could cause as much pleasure as this moment, and I could keep up the pretence all day long if this was how we settle a few scores.

After the longest kiss, he pulls back and whispers, "Do you think we should go again, you know, ram the message home."

By now I'm pretty sure the car park is deserted, but I'm not going to pass this opportunity up and whisper, "They may still be watching, so it could be fun."

Once again, he goes in for the kill and I'm eager prey. In fact, I could do this all evening, it's that good, but after another long kiss that destroys any walls I hide behind, he pulls back and says huskily, "There, that should set the tongues wagging."

I think I float on air as he gallantly holds the door of his car open and I step/fall inside. The car is low to the ground, but I feel as if I'm walking with my head in the clouds. Miles kissed me. Twice. It felt so good, so normal and so delicious, I want to do it again and again.

The man himself joins me and turns the engine on, turning the heat up to warm our chilled feet.

"So, how was your day?"

Groaning, I sink back in my seat. "Tedious, although I had an idea last night thanks to your mum."

He rolls his eyes. "I dread to think what that was."

As I fill him in, I wonder if I'm doing the right thing, because as the words make a sentence it all sounds a little fanciful. However, Miles has obviously been around his mother too long because he nods with approval.

"I think that's a perfect plan. I'm impressed. We will make a Bond girl of you yet. What's next, breaking and entering in the middle of the night to plant your ideas? I'm sure any agent worth her salts would have that covered by now."

"Maybe, but I decided that Royal Mail could save me the effort involved. It left me free to polish my ideas."

"Which are?"

"Later, Mr Bond, a master manipulator never reveals her secrets until the opportune moment."

He laughs and turns the music on low, and the sound of Christmas fills the small space. The bright lights that we pass promise an exciting time ahead, as I see the trees glittering in windows and gardens as we speed through the dusky evening.

It feels special being here with Miles. Like we're a proper couple going to choose gifts for our loved ones, signed from us both. I wonder what that feels like, to be part of a team where your names are uttered as one unit. Miles and Polly wish you a Happy Christmas. Please join Miles and Polly for Christmas drinks. Miles and Polly thank you for their kind gift and Miles and Polly would like to invite you to their wedding.

How I love the sound of that and brush aside the fact this it's all make believe. But I'm here now and can't waste a minute of the time we do have together because I intend on savouring every delicious second of it.

~

THE MALL IS ABSOLUTELY HEAVING. Hordes of shoppers are rushing around in a Christmas frenzy with only one thing on their mind. Christmas shopping. The noise is deafening as their chatter mixes with the music from the speakers, reminding everyone to have a 'Holly Jolly Christmas.' Thinking of my own list, I imagine its nothing like most peoples. I just have to buy for mum, dad, Suze and Jonathan and the usual secret Santa gift for the anonymous person who will be the glad recipient at the annual Sparkle Crackers staff party, traditionally held on the day before Christmas Eve. That sadly is always the highlight of my Christmas because it's the last time I have any fun. Last year I went to mum's new family and spent the day feigning happiness as I watched her new children unwrapping more gifts than I ever received in my lifetime. I had to be content with a Boots voucher because she 'didn't know what I like'.

However, today I am a different woman to that one. Polly Proudlock is a girl who is no longer content to wait for life to dictate her future. She is going out and grabbing something she always knew she wanted.

Miles is wearing that pained look that most men wear when faced with the mammoth task of shopping for anything. He looks around him in confusion and I grin.

"Ok, who's on the list?"

"Mum, dad, Jessica and Freddie. I don't bother with anyone else."

"What about grandparents, friends, anyone else at all?"

"No, I always send my grandparents Fortnum's hampers.

They don't need much these days but love to receive different luxuries to eat and drink."

Once again, my heart softens at the thought of the joy on their faces as they receive a thoughtful gift from their grandson. He laughs softly. "To be honest, Jessica always arranges it. We just transfer our share and send it from the three of us. Minimal effort on our part and maximum brownie points."

Rolling my eyes, I think about his list. "Ok, maybe we should head to John Lewis. I'm pretty sure we could cover most things there."

Miles nods miserably and I laugh to myself. He obviously hates every minute of this and, like most men I know, would have left everything to the last minute if he had his way.

As we walk through the mall, I love looking at the windows of the brightly lit shops, all advertising Christmas in their own special way. They tempt you inside with the promise of finding that perfect gift, and I wonder what it would feel like if money was no object and you could buy anything you liked. Thinking of my own meagre bank balance, I sigh inside. I'd be lucky to spare any change from a £50 note because that's all I've got to spend. Then again, I've always been a bargain hunter and relish the challenge that brings.

Shopping with Miles is a pleasure – for me, anyway. He agrees with any suggestion I make, just keen to get this over with, and we have soon annihilated his list and are ready to find somewhere to eat.

I feel so hungry I wouldn't care if we just grabbed a sandwich from the food court, but Miles apparently has other ideas because he says with relief, "Let's head off, I've booked us a table near the river. There's a great little restaurant there I used to go to with…"

He falters and I say, "Kate?"

"Yes." I hate the anger in his eyes and the distaste on his face as he says her name. For someone who says he's over her, it's obvious he isn't and the shine from my perfect evening diminishes a little as my heart sinks. How can I compete with the love of his life? He loved her and probably still does. I'm a fool if I think this is anything more than it is and so say with a little less enthusiasm, "It's ok, maybe I should be getting home. I've got a letter to write, remember."

Miles looks surprised. "But I thought…"

"It's fine, I'll grab some cheese on toast or something."

I smile brightly and make to leave, and a firm hand pulls me back.

"Not so fast, Miss Galore, you don't get away from me that easily."

As I spin around, I face a worried expression and he says, "I'm sorry."

"For what?"

"For mentioning Kate. I don't want you to think I'm still pining after her."

"Aren't you?"

I raise my eyes and he shakes his head with determination.

"No, I'm not. To be honest, I can't even bear to say her name. I am so angry at what she put my family through and just the mention of her brings it all back. Don't think for a second I still have feelings for her because if I do, they're bitter ones. No, I'm keen to push that memory aside and move on, which I suppose is why I engineered this evening."

I must look confused because he grins and takes my arm. "Come on, the food is good there and it would be a shame to waste our reservation. I'm also keen to find out a little more about you and your plans for this bright and glittering future you have mapped out."

As we walk from the mall, I feel my heart settle a little. Maybe he has moved on and is open to change. Perhaps a chance meeting could turn into something more, I'd like to think so, anyway.

CHAPTER 25

*G*iovanni's is a small trattoria by the river and looks like a magical grotto. Fairy lights twinkle from every tree and are reflected back in the water that swirls in the darkness like an ink pond. Lanterns burn brightly on the brick walls outside and pots of Christmas trees stand proudly at the entrance, guarding a red carpet that could do with a wash. The place itself is charming and the happy chatter of its customers greets us as we stumble in from the cold, bringing with us an icy blast from the weather outside.

A beaming waiter steps forward and says jovially, "Welcome, welcome, have you booked?"

"Yes, the name's Miles Carlton, table for two."

He grabs some menus and asks us to follow him and we are soon seated at a table overlooking the river that is nothing but a black backdrop of darkness outside. The light from the candle on the table reflects in the glass and creates a magical atmosphere. It feels nice being here with Miles and the red-checked tablecloth transports us to Italy as the menu promises a feast of Italian cuisine.

We order some drinks and I settle back in my seat, having immediately decided what I want. Pasta Carbonara with a side salad.

Miles chooses pasta Rigatoni and a side of garlic bread and we sit back and share our drinks, separated by a flickering candle standing proudly in an empty bottle of wine.

"So, tell me, Polly, what are your ideas for Mr Sullivan?"

"Well, your mum gave me some good ones, so I thought I'd start with them. I can't wait to be honest; I really do have so many ideas and think they could work."

He takes a sip of his wine and nods with approval. "Good for you. I'm impressed."

As I look at him something catches my attention from the corner of my eye and I see a familiar face. For a moment I think I'm seeing things and look again, but there's no mistaking the woman laughing from across the restaurant. Susie.

I look at the man she is with and don't recognise him. He looks a little older than her, with greying hair and a face that has aged well. He is dressed in a black suit with a white shirt and red tie and looks distinguished. I see him laughing at something she says and then watch in disbelief as he reaches across the table and takes her hand in his and then raises it to his lips and kisses her fingers. I can't stop staring and Miles looks over his shoulder and says with interest, "Do you know them?"

Leaning forward, I hiss, "That's my flatmate and best friend, Susie. I don't have a clue who she's with, though. She's never mentioned him and I only hope to God it's not that married man she developed feelings for."

Miles looks shocked. "What, the friend you helped out on the night you met me?"

"Yes."

He looks again and then leans in and whispers, "Do you think he's a client?"

"Possibly."

We both look again and I say fiercely, "Don't look."

"You are."

"I know, but I have the bird's-eye view. Should I go over there and say something?"

"Definitely. You have the perfect excuse because you are best friends, it would look strange if you didn't."

"You're right, of course, it's perfectly fine. I'll be right back."

Taking a large gulp of wine, I smile with a bravery I don't feel and head across to my friend. They are deep in conversation with their heads together, and for a moment they don't register that I'm standing there at all. Then the man looks up and says, "May I help you?"

Susie looks up and squeals. "Oh my god, Polly, what are you doing here? Scott, this is Polly, the girl I was telling you about, my bestie."

Her companion looks at me a little more warmly, and I note how his eyes crinkle up at the edges as he grins. "I'm pleased to meet you, Polly, I've heard a lot about you. Will you join us?"

"Um, no, sorry, I'm with someone."

Susie's eyes widen and she mouths, "Batman?"

I nod. "The man himself."

Scott looks a little confused and Susie laughs loudly. "You know, Scott, the one I was telling you about. The man I should have met."

They look over at Miles who is doing a good job of studying his phone and Susie whispers, "He looks hot, just like you described. What's happening with him, are you two…"

"Just friends. Anyway, what about you?"

I stare at her pointedly and she blushes a little, which isn't like her. "Well, um…"

Scott interrupts. "We're a couple."

Susie's eyes are wide as she looks at him in shock. "Do you mean that?"

Now I feel very much in the way, as he says softly, "If you'll have me, that is."

It feels a little awkward to be caught up in what appears to be a major moment in her life, so I back away and say quickly, "I'm sorry, I'll catch you later."

I don't think they notice me, as they stare into each other's eyes and then lean in for a long lingering kiss. I feel a little hot under the collar as I feel the steam hitting me as I walk from their table.

As I sit down Miles says. "Well?"

"Um, I think that's Susie's new boyfriend. He's a little older than I imagined though."

Miles looks around. "I suppose so. Where did she meet him?"

"Probably through the job, like us."

The silence falls between us and I feel a little uncomfortable. I absolutely hate the fact that Miles has paid for my company on at least one occasion and the fact we are still playing the same charade, is leaving me with a bitter taste in my mouth. Even though I really like him, I can't shake the fact he's only here because he wants a business transaction, not a relationship, and suddenly I feel weary. It all felt so exciting, so different, and as if I was one of them. The people that live normal lives with a boyfriend, a life, a purpose. All of this is built on a lie and I am hating every moment of it.

Then a warm hand grasps mine and tugs me across the table. He meets me half way and eyes that appear to hold the secrets of the universe, stare at me with an emotion I haven't seen before when anyone's looked at me.

"Polly Galore."

"Yes." I feel breathless as I wait for something to happen that I can only dream of, and then Miles whispers, "I no longer want to carry on with our deal."

The waves of disappointment crash all around me as his words pour cold water over all my plans. He wants out. Like me, he's having second thoughts and I feel so disappointed I could cry. Instead, I smile bravely. "Oh, ok, that's fine."

"It is?"

He looks a little hurt and I say quickly, "What I mean is, it's fine, I understand. I suppose, like me, you feel bad about lying to your parents. I get that, I would too. No matter, it was fun being your girlfriend while it lasted."

I smile bravely to disguise my feelings and Miles nods. Then he holds out his hand and says politely, "Hi, I don't think we've met, I'm Miles and I would love it if you'd agree to go out on a date with me."

"What?"

I stare at him in shock and he winks. "I saw you sitting here and thought I'd pluck up some courage and go for it. There's something about you that's familiar, have I met you before? Maybe you're a famous actress. I know - you were in that latest Bond movie, weren't you. I must say I'm a big fan."

He grins and I shrug. "I'm sorry, I get this all the time. Men hit on me 24/7 what can I say, it's the by-product of fame."

He nods. "I expect it is, you must be mobbed wherever you go."

"Always."

We share a smile and then I point to the chair he's already sitting in. "Please join me. It appears that I've been stood up, anyway. So, what did you say your name was?"

So, this is it. A new beginning. In one conversation Miles has changed what this is to something much more exciting. I completely forget about Susie and Scott and concentrate instead on the man opposite me who is being charming, sweet and everything I have ever wished for. Maybe dreams do come true and I am witness to that.

We share a perfect evening and at the end of the meal he says gently, "Would you let me escort you home, Polly Proudlock."

"I would like that, thank you."

Reaching across the table, he takes my hand and covers it with his. Then he says softly, "Let's start again, for real this time."

Tears blind my vision as the magic all around me transforms my life completely. He may not be Prince Charming, but he's my superhero.

I think I always knew that.

CHAPTER 26

*D*ear Mr Sullivan

As promised, please find a list of suggestions for your new product line, or should I say, your company transformation product line.

1.   Fill your own crackers. (This is the cheaper option with a name tag to attach to it securing the gift inside.)
2.   Promise cracker (No gift, just a pre-printed card to insert where the customer writes a promise to the recipient. Again, a cheaper option.)
3.   The luxury cracker. (A high-end gift, along with superior hat and meaningful quote. Superior ribbon and packaging, for those customers where cost is not a consideration.)
4.   Cracker advent drawers with snap. (High-end drawers that snap as you open them with a cosmetic treat for the ladies, gadgets for the men and toys for the children. High price point and can be branded to suit a chain of stores or a luxurious brand.)

5.   **Bespoke crackers with own company branding and gift option. (Minimum quantity needed but orders secured in January for delivery by August.)**

6.   **Budget brand. (An updated version of our current offering.)**

As you can see, I have many ideas that with careful planning, could secure a tidy profit for the company. The world demands more luxury now, and people think nothing of paying out for a product of quality. I would pitch the company in the higher end and leave the budget versions to the mass-produced factories in China.

I will be interested to hear what you think.

Best wishes

A concerned and supportive admirer.

I feel a little flustered as I head to the factory, the note in the envelope burning a hole in my pocket. Because of my late night, I missed the morning post and somehow, I need this letter to find its way onto Mr Sullivan's desk. I'm not sure how to approach this and feel the butterflies stirring a storm inside.

I walk slowly past the security point and look for anything that could help me. The post is resting on the desk tied up in a bundle as always, and I wonder if it would give the game away if I offered to deliver it personally. For a moment, I hesitate and as Harry looks up, I see him look at me with interest and so I just smile and carry on walking, kicking myself for not being brave enough to try at least.

It feels like the most important thing in my life to deliver this letter, and so I hang around a bit until I see Mr Sullivan's secretary heading towards the security point. I know I'm late for my shift, but I can't help that and duck into the toilets to wait for her to return.

Leaving the door open a crack, I wait nervously until I hear her heels click past the open door. As she passes, I seize my chance and open the door, which hits her arm causing her to stumble and the pile of letters fall to the ground. I waste no time and say apologetically, "I'm so sorry, Mrs Barrett, I didn't see you. Please, let me help you."

As I drop to my knees and gather the post, I add my own letter to the middle of the pile and thrust them into her hands. "Here you go, you're not injured, are you?"

I look at her anxiously and she smiles. "It's fine, I wasn't looking, anyway."

She heads off and I breathe a sigh of relief. I'm not sure how I pulled that off, but the most important thing is that I did. Thank goodness.

By the time I reach my place on the production line, Richie is waiting and looks unusually angry as he pointedly stares at his watch and says tersely, "I am running out of patience with you, Polly."

The other workers fall silent as they sense a dressing down and I try to apologise. "I'm s…"

"Save your excuses, I've had enough. My office in ten minutes."

He struts off and Marion says sympathetically, "I'm sorry, Polly. He's in a rotten mood today."

Cindy nods. "I heard him telling Rachel off who works on ribbons. She was only a few seconds late and you should have heard him."

Gail looks miserable. "He wasn't himself last night either. Maybe he's worried about our jobs. I wouldn't put it past him, he does think the world of everyone you know. I mean, being management, he is privy to all sorts of secrets. Do you think he knows something?"

The others look horrified and I shrug. "Maybe, I just think I pushed him too far. Don't be surprised if this is the last you see of me."

"I hope not, if it is, you can rest assured we will go on strike."

Marion looks angry and I smile. "It's fine, I can handle Richie – I think."

My smile is as fake as the plastic rings in these crackers, and I leave them and head towards Richie's office. This could be it, the moment when he gives me that written warning and my card is marked. I may not get the opportunity to work on the mezzanine level after all. Then again, if it is, I would march right up to Mr Sullivan and throw myself on his mercy.

As I knock softly on the door to the half office, I feel a little nervous. A gruff voice calls me in and I enter, leaving the door open behind me.

"Close the door."

Richie's voice is curt and I look at him in confusion. "Are you sure, I mean, I'm not sure if that's possible."

His office is not designed to house two people in it, so I'm not sure of the logistics of this, but he just sighs and sits on the edge of his desk, leaving his chair free. "Sit."

My heart thumps as I do as I'm told, and he leans past me and closes the door with a resounding thump. However, he forgets to pull his arm back and just leaves it pressed against the door, bringing him awkwardly close and invading my personal space. I can feel his breath on my face as he whispers, "You've won."

"What?"

I'm not sure what he means and stare at him in confusion,

and he laughs softly and then touches my face lightly, making me jump back in surprise.

"That stunt you pulled last night, arranging for that man to pick you up, it worked."

"What are you talking about?"

I almost think he's going to kiss me and I feel a moment of panic. Instead, he just says softly, "I was jealous. He was kissing my girl; I didn't like it."

"But Gail..."

"Is irrelevant. Last night proved to me that it's you, it's always been you, and I was a fool to let you go."

"But..."

"Kiss me, Polly, tell me you'll come back to me. Let's start again and do things properly this time. I'll end it with Gail, I should never have started it in the first place. Forgive me my darling and I'll spend the rest of my life making it up to you."

Before I know what's happening, he presses his lips to mine and pushes me back in the chair. I have absolutely nowhere to go and feel sick as he takes something I am not offering. I can't even move, let alone speak, and as he groans and pulls me closer, I try to fight back and push him away. Either he doesn't notice, or disregards it because he is a man on a mission and that appears to be me. The only thing left to do is bite down heavily on his lip, and it certainly doesn't taste of cherry lip balm. It tastes of bitterness, despair and hate and the rage that is bubbling up inside me is threatening to send me to prison for murder.

"Bitch."

He pulls back and I note with satisfaction the blood pooling on his lip as he frantically tries to stem the flow. Quickly, I push the chair back and reach for the door handle, saying fiercely, "How dare you assault me like that. I will report you for sexual harassment in the workplace."

"But Polly."

"No buts, how dare you think I'll be happy with that. What about Gail? Yesterday she was the love of your life. Now it's all changed because you hate the fact I've moved on. Well, tough, I have and I'm never going back and certainly not to a creep like you. Stay away from me in the future because if you come near me again, I'm going to Mr Sullivan."

I storm from the half-office like an Amazonian warrior. I feel empowered by rage and leave as a new woman. I will no longer stand by and let people walk over me. I'm better than that, and Richie Banks had better not try anything like that again.

I feel bad for Gail, though. I never thought I would, but Richie was cruel and dismissive of her feelings. All the time I thought they made a sweet couple, it was just a smokescreen. He wasn't invested in their relationship at all. It dawns on me that men like Richie need control. He loved the fact I was upset and probably got a kick from seeing me moping around after him. He probably used Gail to score points and no doubt will do the same to her in the future. Maybe I should forewarn her, but then again, would she listen? She may think I'm stirring trouble again, and we've only just put the awkward atmosphere behind us.

When I head back to the line, the others look at me with concern and I suppose I must look troubled because Cindy gasps, "You poor thing, what did he say, was it awful, are you on a written warning?"

Gail's eyes are wide and she looks bothered and I don't have the heart to be the one to burst her love bubble. Marion just looks angry and I know she would have my back if required, but now is not the time for that. I need to make it all go away because making a scene is not part of my life plan. So, I just smile bravely and shake my head. "It's fine, I'm like a cat with nine lives and will still be here to tell the tale tomorrow."

The relief on the faces of my friends tells me I've done the right thing. I'm not so sure though, would I prefer to be told if something like that ever happened to me? My inner glow of happiness is fading as I worry about the poor girl next to me. Thankfully, I found a new man who is one hundred times better than the old one. I just hope Gail is that lucky.

Thankfully, we don't see Richie for the rest of the shift and as soon as the clock strikes five, I'm off and running. I need to get back to normality because this has been the strangest day. Maybe Susie and I can crack open a bottle of wine and she can tell me what I should do.

CHAPTER 27

*L*uckily, Susie is home when I get there and is curled up on the settee with a glass of wine already. She is watching Elf and I kick off my shoes and grab a glass and join her almost immediately. Sighing, I sink back on the settee and take a huge gulp of wine.

"Bad day?"

She looks at me with sympathy and I groan. "You could say that. Richie cornered me in his office and begged me to come back to him. Then he kissed me against my will."

"He did what?"

Susie is outraged on my behalf and it feels good to be able to offload on someone who is always on my side. "Yes, it was quite a shock I'm telling you, not to mention that I had to work alongside my replacement who could have become my predecessor if Richie got his way."

Susie shakes her head and says angrily, "What a creep. How did it end?"

"I bit his lip and made it bleed, and now I may be infected with creepyitis. What if he has a disease, I wouldn't put it past him? Perhaps I'll turn into a vampire, now I've got blood lust you might not be safe."

For a moment we just share a grin and then she rolls her eyes. "Idiot. Anyway, how did you leave it?"

"I told him if he ever tried that again, I'd report him for sexual harassment. I think it did the trick."

Susie nods her approval and then I remember the man from the pub and say eagerly, "Ok, tell me about Scott, was that his name?"

She blushes and stares at her glass. "Yes."

This is odd. I wonder why she's so cagey, so I try again.

"Things seemed to be going well. Is that the guy who knows Kevin, you know, his boss?"

"No."

"No?" I stare at her in shock because Susie is obviously a fast worker because it's only been a few days and now she's hooked up with a father figure.

Flicking pause on the remote, I say firmly, "Ok, start at the beginning and don't miss a thing. Something's going on and I need all the details."

She looks utterly terrified and my heart sinks. It appears as if she has the weight of the world on her shoulders and I wonder what's going on. Then she begins to sob, madly, loudly and uncontrollably and I am so shocked, the only thing I can do is pat her on the back and murmur words of comfort.

After a while, she stops and sniffs, blowing her nose into a nearby tissue and looks at me through weary eyes.

"I've made a complete mess of things, Polly, and I don't know what to do."

Taking a deep breath, I smile reassuringly. "Tell me everything, it can't be that bad."

"I'm afraid it is. The thing is, as you know, I met Kevin's boss, who sort of went crazy and used my information to haul him in and read him the riot act. The next day Kevin called and threatened me."

"He did what?"

Susie's eyes fill with tears and she sniffs. "He told me to watch out and if his wife got one sniff of this, he would ruin me. He would lodge a complaint with the agency and I wouldn't be safe. He said he would make it his business to ruin my life as I would ruin his if this ever got out. Oh, Polly, it was awful. I felt like such a fool, and yet there was nothing I could do. It wasn't a crime what we did, I couldn't report him to the police, so I just agreed to back off and act as if I'd never met him."

I feel so angry I want to hire a hitman to finish him off. If I knew such a person, I may be tempted but instead I have to calm my rage and say evenly, "Well, at least he's out of your life, you don't need a man like that in it."

"The thing is, I don't feel safe anymore. I am permanently looking over my shoulder just in case he's lurking in the shadows. When I went to work, I half expected to see him stalking me and I just wasn't myself. Then Scott came along."

"Yes, tell me about him, he seems, um, nice."

She nods.

"He is, very nice. He's also very rich and very intense. I met him through the agency. He needed an escort for a function in London. Somebody to help him through a tedious evening, some sort of industry awards ceremony. He's not married and never has time for relationships and prefers his dates like his business. Everything has its place and fits neatly inside a labelled box in his life. He's an interesting character, that's for sure."

I feel a little confused. A character! That's an odd choice of words for someone she professes to have feelings for.

"So, we had a good time at the awards and on the way home we got talking. I told him about Kevin and my fears and he understood. He was very curious about my life, my job, and it felt good to have someone listen and appear interested in me. Well, one thing led to another and well, I suppose I broke my golden rule."

"You didn't…" I stare at her in horror and she nods, looking a little ashamed. "I'm afraid I did. I stayed the night with him and it was nice, actually."

"Nice." She certainly doesn't look like a woman who is happy with her choice and I feel sorry for her when she smiles bravely. "Well, as it happens, Scott is unhappy about things too. He told me he had come to a decision a while ago that he doesn't want to be on his own anymore. He's ready to do the whole relationship thing and that night we saw you and Miles, he told me he wanted that relationship to be with me. He would look after me and we would become a proper couple. You know, the full works, move in, set up home, be an item."

"Are you happy about that because the tears tell me otherwise?"

"Not really." She wipes her eyes and says sadly. "I always thought I'd fall in love and be swept off my feet. You know, the whole fairy tale, the fantasy. Scott is a gentleman, he's nice and good company, but…"

"Something's missing."

"Yes. I don't know, I just feel like another one of his business transactions. A deal made in the back of a taxi on the way back from a business function. There is no passion there, no magic and no romance. He's older than me, so I thought maybe that's what happens. Although I'm feeling happy that I'm not alone anymore, something is telling me I am, alone, I mean. I can just see my future now, married to him, living in luxury and travelling the world."

"Well, now you put it like that…" I grin and she manages to raise a small smile. "The thing is, Polly, it's all so cold. I've no doubt he wants the whole family thing. You know, kids at private school, golf club soirees, the usual stuff rich people like to do and at first, I was sucked into it. Then I keep on watching these romances on tv and my heart feels cold. There's no spark between me and Scott, just friendship really. What am I going to do because on the face of it, it seems like a dream come true, but on the other hand, I want the romance?"

"Then don't go ahead with it, say you've changed your mind and want to take things slowly. Surely, he would understand. How old is he, by the way?"

"48."

"And he's never been married, engaged even?"

"No." She shakes her head. "Seems a little odd don't you think?"

"Not really." I choose my words carefully. "Some men are all about the business. It sounds as if he's done very well for himself and probably concentrated on that instead of a relationship. Perhaps he's realised that there's more to life than the bottom line and has decided to address it. He's chosen an attractive young wife who will provide him with a family, and because he's so successful, he's able to provide a comfortable life for them. It all makes perfect sense to me."

Susie nods thoughtfully. "I suppose if you put it like that, it does."

"But what about you, I think you like the idea, but I'm not sure if he's 'the one?' You know, your soulmate, partner in crime and the love of your life. You're not a business transaction, Susie, you're a young woman with the world at her feet. You can do and be anything you want to be, and is this relationship what you truly want? As for Kevin Potter, I would put him out of your mind, the guy's a coward, picking on a defenceless young girl and putting the fear of God in her. He won't do anything because men like that are bullies and he's just running scared. If he does cross your path again, tell him you have lodged a file with the local police station and if anything happens to you, his door is the first one they'll knock on. Tell him the agency has procedures set in place for creeps like him, and if he comes near you again, you won't hesitate to take it further. That should do the trick, men like that are cowards after all."

Susie smiles through her tears and nods gratefully. "Thanks, Polly, I knew I could count on you. I'm sorry I've been so secretive but it all got a little too much really and I didn't know how to handle it."

"So, what will you do now?"

"I'm not sure. I need some time, so I think I'll just go home for Christmas and consider my options. Scott is heading to his Villa in Florida for most of it. He asked me to join him but I said I had to go home otherwise I'd be disowned by my parents. He didn't seem to mind, so I think I'll take the time apart to really think about my future. Maybe a bit of space will bring clarity."

She says with interest, "What about you and Miles, how are things there?"

A delicious feeling creeps over me at the thought of my new boyfriend. I was certainly the lucky one in all this and can't stop a broad smile from breaking out. "Really good. We are now officially dating and I can't wait to see where this leads. I am planning a bright future, both in my love life and career, and it all seems to be slotting into place, which reminds me, I have a letter to write."

Jumping up, I head to my room as Susie flicks the film back on and the sound of Christmas music invades the room once again.

As I grab my notepaper, I sit on my bed and pen the final letter in my elaborate job application.

Dear Mr Sullivan

Now to the reason for my letters. I would like to put to you a business proposition that will be mutually beneficial.

I would work as your product designer for a period of six months, with an option for a permanent position if my ideas are successful. I would redesign your product and transform your business.

We would start with my boldest idea that I am sure will generate a buzz around Sparkle Crackers that will drive sales.

We launch in the New Year with a campaign that your sales team will promote to all your customers, including your old ones. In every Sparkle Cracker manufactured next year will be a series of golden tickets. These will be in the form of giveaways that promise either a cash reward, a day out somewhere nice, or something along those lines. The only cost to you will be the printing of the golden ticket because I would ask businesses to sign up to provide the reward for you, in exchange for a mention in your marketing material. You would set up a competition page on your website and people could register their prizes there and enter a competition to win a big prize next Christmas. I am sure you can see the benefits of this for you as a business and for your partners. I can see press interest, a huge advertising campaign, and something that sets you aside from the competition. You would be the first cracker manufacturer to take things to a new level which will elevate your business to that of a luxury brand, rather than one struggling to hold on.

In all of this I have kept your costs to a minimum, although there will initially be more of an outlay as you create a luxury brand. With the correct orders in place, you could prove to the bank your business is a viable option and secure the money you need to make it all happen.

If you like my ideas and are willing to give me a chance, you only have to announce it at the staff Christmas party and I will step forward. If not and you hate everything I've written, just carry on as normal and forgive me for daring to think I know better than you.

Yours hopefully,

A friend

CHAPTER 28

a few days later, Miles picks me up to go to his parents' for lunch. I feel a little nervous because apparently his brother and sister will be there and I'm keen to make a good impression. Susie has been spending her evenings with Scott and has decided to put her work on hold with the agency for a few weeks, which worries me a little. She needs the money after all and stands to earn a lot of it with the run up to Christmas. It's always a busy time of year, but she told me that Scott was subsidising her wages so she could spend all her time with him.

The whole situation is worrying me because she is putting her brave face on, but I'm not sure if she really wants this at all. She's acting like she does, and even Jonathan voiced his concerns when I met him in the hallway the other day. He told me he had serious doubts that they would last because only true love seals a deal for eternity. I have to agree with him and know that what I have already with Miles is so different to her relationship. I can't wait to see him and when we aren't together, we speak on the phone for hours. He's busy working on some takeover bid for a client from their offices in Harpenden. I'm busy with project mezzanine level and trying to just get through the day by avoiding Richie as much as possible, which is working out rather well as he is spending more time over at the ribbon end of the business.

So, when the doorbell rings, I am more than happy to launch myself into Miles's arms and kiss him as if he's been at sea for six months.

Laughing, he pulls back and says happily, "That's a welcome and a half, I'm pleased to see you too."

"Good, I would be worried if you weren't."

We grin stupidly at each other, and then he reaches for my hand. "Shall we?"

"Lead the way, Batman."

We head off and once again I feel nervous. I love his parents and am looking forward to seeing them again, but his siblings are unchartered territory. What if they disapprove?

Miles is also a little quiet, and I wonder what his relationship with his brother is like now. He must also be feeling a little worried because, after all, the whole reason for us getting together in the first place was to repair his relationship with his family.

Our journey today is a little quieter which only fuels my anxiety, and after a while, I say nervously, "Tell me about your brother, what does he do for a living?"

"He's an architect."

"Wow, that's impressive."

"It is." Miles sounds proud, which is a good sign, and I carry on prying. "Where does he live?"

"Surrey. He works out of a converted barn in Gomshall and has built up quite a business. He is always busy and the work never seems to dry up."

"What does he design?"

"Houses mainly, you know, projects, extensions, new builds, that sort of thing."

"And your sister?"

His voice warms a little and he laughs. "Jessica's a journalist. She works for one of those women's magazines, you know, the gossip ones. It suits her because she's so nosey and loves nothing more than gossiping. You should hear her and mum when they get together. They don't come up for air and dad ends up taking me and Freddie to the pub for some peace."

I laugh. "I'm impressed, your family is very successful, your parents must be very proud but also a little disappointed."

"Why?"

"What about your father's business, do you think he wanted one of you to follow in his footsteps?"

Miles shrugs. "Possibly, but my parents aren't like that. They just want us to be happy and do whatever does the trick. Dad earns a good living but wouldn't expect us to join him if it wasn't what we wanted."

"Have you ever been tempted?"

"Not really. I like what I do and if I worked with my dad, we would fall out pretty quickly."

"Surely not." I picture Miles's lovable father and can't see it somehow, and he laughs loudly. "Don't be fooled by his lovable rogue act, Polly. That man hasn't got where he is today by being soft. He's hard, irritable and ruthless at work. Credit to him though, he leaves it behind when he comes home at night. Mum would murder him if he didn't. We all kind of like that side to him and are keen to have him as a father, not a boss."

"That makes sense."

Thinking about Miles and his family restores my faith a little. They are everything I thought a real family was, and now I understand why Miles was keen to convince them he was happy. It seems that family means more to them than anything, and who wouldn't be impressed by that.

Once again, I feel the thrill as we pull up outside Pauline and Elvis's amazing home. If I could have a home like this one day, I would consider myself very fortunate indeed. It makes me feel so happy as I look at the beautiful wreath hanging on the white door that looks clean and polished. The light up reindeers either side of it are guarding an impressive portico and the lights that are strung under the eaves promise a little piece of magic when the darkness falls. The crunch of gravel as we pull up alerts the inhabitants to our arrival and the door is flung open revealing an excited Pauline wearing her Cath Kidston apron with pride. She shouts, "They're here. Elvis they're here."

Miles grins and says under his breath, "Brace yourself, Polly."

Laughing, I exit the car and am soon folded into a warm hug from both his parents.

"Polly, babe, come on in, it's bloody freezing out here. Look at that thin coat you've got on, it's not fit for purpose. I've got the wood burner going and I'll make you a nice cup of tea. Elvis take Polly's coat and don't just chuck it in the cupboard like you usually do."

Miles rolls his eyes as I am propelled inside, and I love every minute of it. Pauline makes me feel so welcome, unlike my own family, and I appreciate every word she says. This is what I imagine a family should be like, and if I could live here with them, I would love every minute of it.

I am interested to see a woman sitting at the kitchen island unit looking at me with interest. She's an attractive girl with long blonde hair curled at the ends and twinkling blue eyes and is dressed immaculately in tight jeans and an oversized jumper. She smiles with interest as I head into the room.

"Jess honey, this is Polly, you know, Miles's girlfriend, isn't she pretty?"

I feel myself blushing as Jessica smiles, "Yes, she is." She stands and says warmly, "Hi, I'm Jessica but you can call me Jess. Come and sit with me and I'll tell you all my brother's secrets."

She squeals as he heads across and sweeps her off her feet, spinning her around until she cries out, "Stop it, I'm going to be sick."

Watching them is like watching one of those feel-good American movies. The perfect family with the perfect life. I'm so envious because I always wanted a brother or sister. Someone to share my life with and share a history. Once again, it reinforces how lonely my own life is, but I'm not allowed to wallow in self-pity here because Pauline shouts, "Miles put your sister down, what must Polly think of you? Anyway, Polly, I've been busy since you were here last and made these gorgeous Christmas cards. I've made some for you too if you want them. Jessica has twelve and so do the boys. Hopefully it helps a little."

Jessica catches my eye and pulls a face, which makes me giggle.

Elvis comes in and booms, "I could murder a lager, got any of those German ones Pauline?"

"In the fridge, get it yourself."

Jessica looks at me with interest. "So, mum tells me you work in a cracker factory, that must be so interesting."

"Not really, but it could be."

"Tell me, what are you planning?"

Her eyes light up when I tell her of my letters and Pauline joins in. "Oh my god, that's genius. It worked for me like I told you, ooh, let me know how it all goes, I bet it works."

Jessica nods enthusiastically. "Me too, you know, I could write a story on it, create some interest in the media."

"Wow, that would be amazing would you really do that?"

"Sure, anything to help."

Elvis shouts from across the room, "Freddie's here, his car's just nearly taken out the rhododendron."

"Nothing new there then." Pauline rolls her eyes as they both head off to meet him.

CHAPTER 29

*J*essica watches her parents leave and then turns her attention to me and I don't miss her razor sharp stare assessing me. Not in a bad way though, I guess she's making sure she approves of her brother's choice because I'm sure she's only got his best interests at heart after the last time.

She says tentatively, "Have you told Polly about…"

"Kate."

She winces, and I feel immediately on edge at the mention of the woman who almost tore this family apart.

Miles sighs. "To be honest, Jess, Kate is in the past and I'm happy to leave her there. As long as Freddie's happy, I'm happy."

"What, even if they were still together?"

"Even then." She shakes her head and he says tightly, "It's true. Since it happened, I haven't missed her, not really. If anything, I'm glad I found out what she was like before it went any further. My only concern now is that Freddie's ok because I know how he must have felt when she ditched him for his best friend. Are they still together, do you know?"

I feel my heart pounding ten to the dozen as my mind goes into overdrive. Is he asking because he still has feelings for her? Would he get back with her given half a chance? As always, I picture the worst and then he places his arm around me and says softly, "She did me a favour because if I was still with her, I wouldn't have met Polly. She's made me realise there's better. *She's* better and I thank God it all happened."

Jessica smiles. "I'm happy for you. It all worked out in the end."

"What about you, I thought you were seeing someone?"

"Were is correct. We split up a couple of weeks ago. To be honest, he started to bore me and became really clingy. I couldn't move without him asking where I was going, and it was a little stifling, really. Never mind, there's always a backup plan and I'm 'talking' to a guy I met on Dream Beginnings, he seems nice and we may even meet up one day."

"Don't let mum know you're Internet dating, she'll blow a fuse."

"I'm not stupid."

"That's a matter of opinion."

They grin at each other and I laugh to myself. Dream Beginnings, I know of it well. Susie loves the site and is always trawling through the men on offer looking for her mister right. I wonder what went wrong for her? I suppose Kevin Potter went wrong for her and it's thrown her off balance.

Thinking of it, Susie would love Jessica. They appear to be from the same mould and I'm sure have lots in common.

Suddenly, Pauline enters the room and rolls her eyes as she says loudly, "Freddie's here, plus one."

We look with interest as two people follow her in, minus Elvis who is probably on cloakroom duty.

Freddie is much like his brother. Tall, dark and gorgeous and is wearing a winter looking jumper and jeans along with a broad smile on his face as he sees his family. The woman with him is certainly beautiful, making me feel a little inadequate. She has long brown hair that is styled to professional standards, and her make-up is immaculate. Her clothes look expensive and puts my own appearance to shame. Regretting my choice of jeans and a fluffy jumper, I wish I had dressed up for the occasion as she has. Her dress is knitted and falls to her knee and looks like the softest grey cashmere and her boots appear to be made out of expensive leather. Beautiful delicate jewellery finishes off the outfit and she clutches a small bag that has my eyes popping with envy when I see the exclusive label.

Freddie looks at me with interest and I shrivel up with embarrassment. He is probably judging me and finding me a very poor alternative in comparison to his own glamorous companion but he seems friendly enough and smiles as he extends his hand, "Hi, you must be Polly, I'm Freddie, the number one son and most adored of the family."

He winks and Miles rolls his eyes before saying charmingly, to Freddie's date "Hi, I'm Miles, the more handsome of the Carlton brothers, I'm sorry I didn't catch your name."

"Annabella."

She holds out her hand and I watch Miles share a fairly awkward handshake with her. In fact, it's more of a brush of hands because she drops hers almost immediately and looks at Jessica with interest. Jessica smiles and says kindly, "I'm Jessica, the only sane one in the family. It's good to meet you Annabella, how did you two meet?"

Elvis interrupts by heading in and saying irritably, "That bloody hook's fallen down again, I told you not to hang so much stuff on it, Pauline."

"Shut up moaning, Elvis, we'll get Jimmy Handy in, he'll sort it."

Miles catches my eye and grins. "Jimmy Handy is the

local handyman. He's in huge demand because he doubles as a male stripper in the evening. I'm sure you get why he's so popular. Knowing mum, she's done it on purpose just as an excuse to call him in."

Pauline grins as Elvis rolls his eyes and I stifle a giggle. Annabella, however, looks a little disgusted and my heart sinks. Oh dear.

"So, Bella, babe, what can I get you to drink?"

As ever Pauline cuts to the chase and Annabella says firmly, "A white wine spritzer made with a dash of soda and a hint of lime would be amazing, Mrs Carlton and please, call me Annabella, I do so hate abbreviated names."

I dare not look at anyone, least of all Pauline and Freddie says quickly, "I'll have a lager, mum."

"Frederick." Annabella's voice is laced with disapproval. "If you're drinking, I'll just stay on soda. We can't both drink if we're driving."

Jessica stiffens beside me and Pauline opens her mouth to say something but Miles gets in first and says quickly, "So, what do you do for a living, Annabella?"

"I'm an entrepreneur business woman with multiple strings to my bow."

Freddie says proudly, "Yes, Annabella has a jewellery business that's doing well online. She also has a blog and is in the process of writing a book on business."

Annabella nods and turns to Jess. "If you send me your email, I'll send you a copy to download. It's all about empowering the woman of today to make the right decisions and be successful in her own right, while maintaining a strict work to home life balance."

I feel a little excluded as does Pauline by the look on her face and Jessica says awkwardly, "Oh, thanks, I'll take a look."

Annabella casts her disapproving eye over me and says,

"What do you do for a living, I'm sorry, I didn't catch your name?"

"Um, Polly."

"Interesting, is that short for Pollyanna by any chance?"

"No, just Polly."

"Shame, Pollyanna is one of those names that immediately makes a person memorable."

Pauline says quickly, "Well, I like the name Polly. It's sweet."

I can tell Annabella has rubbed Pauline up the wrong way just by the look she's giving her, but Annabella doesn't seem to notice, or care and without even waiting for an answer to her question, looks around and openly stares at the immaculate kitchen.

"No need to ask what you do, Mrs Carlton. Your home is a credit to you, or do you employ a cleaner?"

"Just a few thousand." Pauline is tight-lipped and we all laugh because she's not joking, they do.

Elvis laughs loudly. "Yes, my Pauline could run rings around my employees. Best cleaner I've ever met and my inspiration. Do you remember kids in the early days when mum insisted on training the workers? If she had her way, I'd be bankrupt inside a fortnight. Only the best products and maximum time spent on the job. No, I had to keep her away to protect our profits because she's a perfectionist."

Annabella smiles faintly and sips her drink, looking as if she would rather be anywhere else.

After a while, Freddie says brightly, "Come on, Annabella, I'll show you around."

He pulls her up and she throws him a strained look, although the rest of us throw him a grateful one as he guides her from the room.

As soon as the door's closed, Pauline pulls a face and whispers, "Where did he find her?"

171

Miles shrugs. "He told me they met when he designed her parent's extension. Apparently, they have a massive house in Guildford and are rolling in money."

"What does her father do?"

"Runs a bank, or something along those lines. I've heard of him, he's a big shot in the city, Freddie's done well for himself."

"That's a matter of opinion."

Pauline looks weary and Elvis places his arm around her shoulders. "Don't worry, love, the poor girl is probably over-whelmed. It's a lot to handle when you meet someone's family. Look at Polly there, she must have felt the same when she first came here."

Pauline sniffs. "Not our Poll, she slid into place like she was meant to be here, not that one. I hope he wakes up and changes her for something better."

Jessica bursts out laughing. "She's not a bag of shopping up for exchange. As long as she makes Freddie happy, does it really matter what we think?"

"Is he happy though?"

Miles shrugs. "I hope so."

His eyes find mine and the look he shoots me melts my soul and the room fades into the background as we share a moment. This is so right because of him. He makes it easy to fit in because he makes me feel as if I'm the most important person in the room. They all do, even though I'm way out of their league. Annabella could learn a lot from these people because even though financially we are all probably out of her league, emotionally we are far above her.

or once I am pleased to leave Pauline and Elvis's amazing home, and it's because of the awkward atmosphere Annabella brings to a room.

Miles sighs with relief as soon as we exit the impressive gated driveway. "Thank God that's over. She was horrific."

"I agree. It was awful the way she kept on correcting Freddie. Oh, Frederick, don't place your elbows on the table, oh Frederick, don't speak with your mouth full, oh Frederick, can you fetch my wrap I'm feeling a chill. Goodness, what on earth does he see in her?"

Miles nods. "It's mum I feel sorry for. Dad couldn't care less but mum is desperate for us to be happy, meet someone and produce the next generation."

I stare at him in shock and he grins. "Buckle up, baby, a few months in and mum will be planning our wedding, closely followed by a baby shower."

"I'm sorry, what did you say?" I feel a little giddy and he laughs. "You watch, she'll start dropping hints into the conversation. She's been on her best behaviour up until now, but soon she'll be leaving wedding magazines strategically placed all around the house and discussing friends of hers whose children have made their mums the happiest women alive by producing grandchildren. She'll start taking you shopping and suggesting venues, and she'll be nagging me to make an honest woman of you."

"She will?" I feel a little faint and yet hopeful at the same time. Am I desperate to pray that she gets her wish? In fact, I can think of nothing I'd love more and Miles says softly, "Sounds good, doesn't it?"

I look at him in surprise, "You're not…"

"Of course not." He grins. "No, when I propose to you, Polly Galore, it will be something James Bond would be proud of."

He reaches across and grasps my hand and a delicious shiver passes through me as I contemplate my life beside him. If miracles really are a thing, I'm experiencing one now because Miles Carlton is my miracle and I am reluctant to think of a time when he isn't in my life.

Miles drops me home and it feels wrong to leave him behind. Then again, I feel nervous to invite him in because there is a level still pending in our relationship that thrills me and scares me at the same time – intimacy. If Susie isn't at home, what if things get a little out of hand? Am I ready for this? In my heart I am, but my mind is still issuing warnings. Keep something back, keep the mystery alive, but I don't want to. I rushed into a sexual relationship with Richie almost the next day, and my feelings were nowhere near as strong as the ones I feel for Miles. But what if it changes things? What if he gets bored and leaves? I can't bear the thought of it and as always when I'm stressing out, I start to bite my lip and Miles says softly, "Polly."

"Um, yes, Miles?"

"Stop worrying."

"How do you know I'm worrying?"

"Because you bite your lip and go quiet on me. You get wrapped up in worry and every emotion shows on your face. It's fine, I'm in no hurry to move this on, we've got the rest of our lives to look forward to and I want it to be right."

He reaches over and pulls me to face him, and I see the soft look in his eyes that melts every defence I've put in place. "I just want to tell you that I think I'm falling in love with you, Polly Galore. You're the Robin to my Batman, the Bond girl to my 007. You are the person I think about first when I wake and last thing at night. The memory of you stays with me when you're not there, and I look forward to spending time with you. I love how you make my parents happy and slot into my life as if you've always been there. I suppose what I'm saying is, stay with me, Polly, be my girl-friend for real this time and let's see where we end up."

"But how?"

He looks confused and I say sadly, "I feel the same, Miles, everything you said is true for me too but there's an elephant in the room that we need to discuss."

"What is it?"

I feel bad as Miles looks so worried and I say gently, "You live in London and I live in Slip End. What happens when the snow melts and you head back there? You love your life in London and I am planning a future here. One of us will have to give something up and I don't want to ask that of you. For the first time in my life, I have something exciting I want to pursue. I want to see if I can make a difference and win that job at Sparkle Crackers. I want you to be happy too and above everything, I want this, us - you. How can we make it work?"

Miles looks as worried as I feel and then says firmly, "We'll make it work. I'll spend my weekends here and during the week we'll facetime in the evenings. Once we've estab-lished ourselves, we'll rethink the situation. Perhaps I could work nearby, or commute. Lots of people do, it would be worth it to spend more time with you."

Everything this man says settles my heart. He always says exactly the right thing and makes me feel like the most desired woman alive.

In the distance we hear the soulful singing of some carollers at a house nearby and the pure magic of the situation makes my heart flutter.

Miles leans forward and kisses me softly, and I absolutely love it. I could stay here all night doing just this with the carollers serenading us, but even I have my limits in midwinter so I say in a whisper, "Come on, I'll make you a coffee."

Hand in hand, we head inside where the central heating has warmed the flat, making it feel welcome and cosy. Susie is out, so I light a few candles and flick on the kettle. Then Miles and I snuggle up together and watch Christmas films until the candle burns low and we fall asleep, wrapped in a duvet on the settee.

CHAPTER 31

*N*ever again. My back is absolutely killing me and as romantic as it was, I am never going to spend the night on the settee again. Miles looked equally sore when he left for work, and I just managed to grab some toast and shower before heading off for the gruelling day ahead. At least there's only a few more days until Christmas, so the mood is a holiday one where we listen to Christmas songs and sing along while tucking into one of the many tubs of sweets that have been gifted to us from well meaning customers.

However, as I drag myself in from the cold, I am met by a stern gaze. Richie is waiting for me and says curtly, "Follow me, Polly."

My heart sinks as I do as he asks and head towards the dreaded cubby hole.

This time he doesn't ask me to close the door and instead sits on his chair looking at me with a slightly imperious smirk.

"I'm sorry, Polly, but it's not good news."

"What isn't?"

My heart starts thumping as I wait for the punch line, and Richie is obviously relishing this moment because he couldn't look any happier if he tried. He is trying to disguise it though and tries to look remorseful, but I can tell he is loving every minute of this.

"I'm sorry to say that your name is on the next list of redundancies. I'm afraid there won't be a job here for you next year and the day before Christmas Eve will be your last one."

"Are you serious?"

My heart plummets like a balloon with sand and I feel winded. Redundant, just before Christmas, I'm too late.

He nods in a patronising way while trying to disguise the smirk on his face.

"I'm afraid Mr Sullivan asked me for a list of people who I felt should be included in the next batch. We can only keep a skeleton staff and need out best people. Every department is cracking down and I need to come up with a list of people to go. As you know, we have had our differences, but I did not let them influence my decision."

I snort and he shakes his head. "I thought you would disagree and that disappoints me, Polly. Surely you should know that I am a fair man and business comes first. Now, you have the next few days to say your goodbyes and leave with dignity. I'm sorry it has to be this way, but I'm sure you can see I had no other choice."

It appears that the conversation is over and I turn to walk away, feeling like a discarded piece of wrapping. Three years and it's over. I will never get the chance to rise to the dizzy heights of the mezzanine level unless Mr Sullivan saves me at the final hour and calls me forward at the Christmas party. I still have that hope at least, but for how long? If they are still cutting staff, things are very bad indeed. I've left it too late.

The others look up with surprise as I make my way to my position beside them on the production line, and even the merry Christmas song on the radio does nothing to lift my spirits. This is it; I'm done and I never thought it would hurt so bad.

Marion is first to notice something is definitely up and says quickly, "What's happened love, are you ok?"

"Not really, I've just been made redundant."

They all gasp and Cindy cries, "Oh my god, I'll be next, I just know it. Poor Polly, what happened?"

I fill them in and Gail looks astonished. "But I thought that was it, Richie never mentioned anything. This is so unexpected."

"Yes, it was for me too."

Nobody knows what to say, and I'm not sure I even want to talk about it. It feels like the biggest rejection ever and for a girl used to rejection it still hurts.

By the time it's morning break, the news has made its way around the factory and apparently, I wasn't the only one. Richie was right about that at least, and one person from every department has been given the cruellest Christmas present. Sadly, Cindy's boyfriend Darren has also suffered the same fate and there are many worried faces trying hard to keep it together as we all contemplate the end of what was once a profitable business. No wonder Mr Sullivan always looked so worried. He will have been trying everything to save this place, but it appears even he's too late.

Just when I thought things couldn't get any worse, they do.

JUST AFTER LUNCH, Richie appears and calls Gail away. Cindy looks horrified and says, "Oh no, not Gail too."

Marion snorts. "More like a passion break knowing him. There's a reason he chooses girls to date from the production line, sorry Polly, he has a steady booty call any time he wants. That man disgusts me."

She shakes her head and stuffs her crackers angrily, and it makes me laugh.

"What's so funny?"

She looks up in surprise and I grin. "You actually, those poor crackers, it looks as if you're taking it out on them. Just think though, these could be the last crackers we ever stuff."

For a moment we realise the sadness of our situation. Ordinarily we hate our jobs, but faced with losing it, a very different emotion takes its place. Nostalgia is kicking in and we are soon sharing stories of funny moments from the past that lift our spirits for a little while at least. Then my world is torn apart as Gail returns looking so excited, she can barely speak.

"Oh my God, you are not going to believe what just happened?"

We all share a look and Marion says quickly, "You were caught in a compromising position by security?"

We giggle as Gail shakes her head furiously. "No, I said you are *not* going to believe this."

We all laugh because actually the thought of them being caught is probably more believable than actually enjoying a shift and Cindy says with excitement, "What's happened?"

"I'm being promoted."

Gail's eyes shine and we stare at her in surprise. "To what?"

"Miss Constable's job. Can you believe it, I'm so excited?"

"But how?" My voice shakes because this is unexpected. Surely Mr Sullivan has seen my letters. Then it dawns on me that maybe he hasn't. Perhaps they never reached 'his eyes only' and they were destroyed. My sure fire promotion plan never got off the ground and to top it all, the woman who stole my boyfriend has now stolen my job as well.

"But how, when was this decided?" Marion asks my unanswered question for me and Gail claps her hands. "I know, mad, isn't it? Richie told me a few days ago that Miss Constable handed in her resignation. He told me on the sly that he would put in a good word for me. Well, it worked because Mr Sullivan was so enthusiastic. He told me I was perfect for the role and all my energy and enthusiasm for the job will make Sparkle Crackers sparkle again. Well, I can't wait, I start after Christmas."

My heart sinks. So, that's it, the final nail in the coffin, I'm done. Richie had the last laugh and ultimate revenge and used his position to push his girlfriend up the ladder past me. It's almost too much and I can't think straight.

As Gail chatters on about her new role and where she will buy her clothes, I tune out. This is a disaster. Maybe I should move to London and find a job there. At least I would be with Miles, but doing what and am I prepared to give up my dreams at the first hurdle?

CHAPTER 32

*S*usie makes it home that evening and I tell her what happened. She's so upset for me and together we crack open a bottle of wine and sniff our way through it, trying to come up with a solution. Susie is also at a crossroads and just can't seem to make a decision. Scott is still keen apparently and has asked her to move in with him. On the face of it she seems happy with that, but is it the right move for her? I also have the offer of moving to London with Miles, and is this the end for us in Slip End? Two girls with so much to look forward to, separated by different directions in different towns. Scott lives in a posh area of Harpenden and Susie would certainly have a good life with him. I would be with Miles, but in both our cases something is missing.

I almost can't face heading into work for my penultimate shift, and only the thought of meeting Miles afterwards is keeping me going. Tonight, he has tickets to go ice skating and I finally get my wish. I should be excited about that, but I can't shake the knot that is forming inside as I wonder what the new year will bring.

It's almost unbearable being at Sparkle Crackers now. It

was bad enough when Gail chatted incessantly about Richie, but now it's *my* job that is her sole topic of conversation. It's hard to hear but I try to act pleased for her. After all, she didn't know about the letters, it's not her fault.

Miles rang earlier and asked to meet at my flat. Something has come up apparently, and he won't be free to meet me at five. As I make my way home, I'm almost tempted to cancel and take to my bed instead. I just want to wrap myself in my duvet and pretend none of this is happening. I don't feel as if I'm good company and I don't want to drag Miles down to my level.

Suze is wrapping presents on the kitchen table when I get there and seems a little brighter. "Hey, let me make you a cup of tea, I'm due a break from all this wrapping."

I smile gratefully and look in wonder at the amazing creations she has obviously spent all day making. "Susie, you have a talent for gift-wrapping, will you do mine?"

"Love to, it keeps me from going mad."

I follow her into the kitchen and perch on the counter as she busies herself making the tea. "Any news?"

She shakes her head. "Nothing's changed. I'm heading home on Christmas Eve and am using the time to consider my options. How about you?"

"Not sure. I keep on hoping for a Christmas miracle. I mean, surely things can't get any worse?"

She hands me the tea and smiles reassuringly. "You'll be fine, you always are. Nothing can defeat you, Polly Proudlock, you're a force of nature."

I nod. "Maybe this is fate telling me I was going in the wrong direction, anyway. Perhaps I was always meant to leave Sparkle Crackers and maybe move to London. I expect this is written in the stars and I'll find an amazing job there and never look back."

"Sure, you will, change is just around the corner for both of us, it will all work out in the end."

The phone rings interrupting our conversation and with a sinking feeling, I see my mum's number on the screen. Pulling a face, I answer it and say sweetly, "Hi mum."

"Ah, Polly, thank God you are home. When you arrive on Christmas Eve, I don't suppose you'll pick up a few things on your way. I'm seriously stressing out here. I need one of those Christmas Eve boxes, you know, the sort you fill with lovely treats to keep them excited on Christmas Eve. I was let down by my online order and they sent three instead of four and now they've sold out with no hope of getting one. Also, I've run out of Sellotape, who knew four children could receive so much at Christmas. I would go myself, but I'm elbow deep in flour and baking and just won't have time. Also, Graham wondered if you wouldn't mind grabbing his dry cleaning when you pass the shop on your way from the station. I would offer to pick you up but we have a drinks party at the neighbours to attend and will probably be out when you arrive."

Why do I feel like this is just another slap in the face? In fact, I think life is enjoying slapping me around a little too much at the moment and so, I take a deep breath and say calmly, "I'm sorry mum, you'll have to arrange something else, I have other plans this Christmas."

For a moment there's silence on the other end and then she says in a tight voice, "Excuse me, what did you say?"

Susie's eyes are wide as she gives me the thumbs up and a little bit of courage as I say with more determination. "I've been seeing someone and his family want me to spend Christmas with them here in Harpenden. It was never confirmed that I was spending Christmas with you, you just assumed I would be. I'm sorry mum but you'll have to make other arrangements for your stuff."

"But who will help me, what will I do without you?"

Just when I thought I couldn't feel any lower, my mum delivers the last hurtful blow. "I'm sorry mum I'm sure you'll cope."

"But Polly, you always come for Christmas, it's expected."

I take a deep breath and try not to slam the phone down in a rage. "Don't you want to hear about me, mum, who I'm dating, my job, my life - anything?"

She falters a little. "Of course, it's just that, well, I thought we'd catch up when you got here. You know I always rely heavily on you at Christmas Polly, this is a little rude of you cancelling at the last minute, you could have told me sooner."

"I'm sorry mum but I'm not in the mood to celebrate, anyway. I've lost my job and am feeling rather low as it happens."

"Lost your job, that's terrible, how will you afford the rent? I'm sorry darling, you know I would love to help, but I have no spare cash to give you. It's all tied up with direct debits, etc, etc. You could always move in here I suppose, but we turned the spare room into a study for Graham. He needs somewhere to work without the chaos that having four children brings and needs the quiet space. Maybe your father can help, have you heard from him?"

"No, I haven't."

"Typical, he was always missing in action even before he joined the Navy. Well, don't expect any help from him, he's always been unreliable."

I can hear voices in the background and she says quickly, "Listen, I've got to go, we're heading out to the Pantomime, maybe you should rethink your decision and come here. You need to be around family at a time like this and take your mind off things. I'll keep you busy and we'll work out a plan."

She cuts the call and I realise she never even asked about my new boyfriend. In fact, knowing her, she couldn't care less and was just using my misery to secure her annual slave for Christmas.

Susie looks sympathetic. "I'm sorry Polly."

"It's fine, she'll never change. The thing is, Suze, through the whole of that conversation it was like talking to a stranger. In fact, my mum has always been a stranger to me because she never really showed me much interest. Now I'm branching out on my own, she doesn't like it. She never even asked about Miles and his family she was so wrapped up in her own. Her new family means everything and I'm just a reminder of a past relationship that went wrong."

"I'm sure she doesn't mean it. Maybe you should tell her how you're feeling, I bet she'd be shocked."

"Its fine, I'm used to it but one thing's for sure, I'm not going there for Christmas. The last thing I want is to be reminded that my mum is a much better one to her new family than she ever was to me."

Looking at the clock on the wall, I say quickly, "I need to change, Miles will be here in a minute, we're heading out ice skating."

"That's great, you lucky thing, I wish I was going. I just don't feel Christmassy this year."

"Maybe you could come with us, I'll ask him."

She holds up her hand. "It's fine, I'm happy to stay and wrap and watch a Hallmark movie. Bring your presents out and I'll wrap them too, it will keep me busy and take my mind off things."

As I get ready, I think about my mum and that conversation. I try not to let it affect me but she is my mum after all and we only get one of those. I wonder why she has always put me behind her latest family. Surely, she wants a good relationship with her only blood relative. Thinking of Jess and Pauline and Susie and her own mother, I feel bitter that I will never have that same bond with my own one. Even my father hasn't called for at least a month and as always, Christmas is the time of year I feel rejected the most. Now I'm an adult, they think I'm off their hands and able to cope. I'm not. I'm still that child inside who wants someone to kiss me and make everything good again. One thing's for sure, I will learn from their mistakes and be the best mum possible to my own children, or die trying.

CHAPTER 33

I love ice skating. This was just the tonic I need, and holding Miles's hand as we glide along the ice is the best remedy for an empty heart I could have wished for. It feels as if I'm living in a Christmas card scene, as we laugh and enjoy the coldest of pastimes.

Planet Ice is buzzing with happy people all enjoying an activity that is a little scary and yet so much fun. At first, I was nervous but soon found my skating feet and now I feel like Jayne Torvill holding onto Christopher Dean. Wrapped in my padded jacket that was a bargain from the local charity shop, I hold Miles's gloved hand as we skate around the rink to loud throbbing music, trying to avoid the human traps that fall at our feet at a split second's notice.

I can forget all my problems when I'm with Miles because he makes life interesting. He's always got a smile on his face and is good company, and nothing else matters as long as I have him by my side. He has rescued Christmas; in fact, he has rescued me because I see a spark of hope in my future now that I'm walking there with him.

Our session ends and we head to the little café for a

warming hot chocolate, although to be honest, I am feeling as if I'm having one of those hot flushes you hear people talking of.

Shrugging out of my jacket, I say in astonishment, "Who knew ice would make you feel so hot?"

Miles grins. "I know, weird isn't it."

He sips his drink as I offload my problems onto him and looks thoughtful. "It's not so bad."

"It is from where I'm sitting."

Reaching across the table, he grasps my hand and I love how warm his hands are courtesy of the steaming mug of chocolate he has been gripping so hard.

"Come to us for Christmas and you never know, Santa may deliver you a different kind of present this year."

"Do you think, I mean, he's busy treating the boys and girls, he may be a little short on miracles."

Miles shrugs. "What about your mum, do you think she'll be upset if you don't show up?"

"I expect so, but only because she won't have someone to wash up, help prepare the meals and generally order around until I leave. My mum is selfish and always has been. Not that she would agree. She thinks she's an amazing mum and she is, to the four children who think she's wonderful."

"What happened to her last husband?"

"He met someone else and moved her out and the new model in. Mum went to live with a friend of hers before she found Graham in the school playground. She's been married to him for three years now and I think they're doing well, at least I hope they are."

"And your dad?"

"He's ok and always seems happy when I get my monthly duty call. To be honest, I can't remember the last time I saw him, he's a virtual stranger to me."

"That must hurt."

"A little, but I'm used to it by now. You see, Miles, it's always just been me growing up and now I'm an adult I've had to make my own way and I'm kind of used to it. It does hurt though when I see my mum being an amazing one to someone else's children. I feel denied something I thought every child had a right to. *Your* mum is everything I imagined a mum to be, and it's restored my faith a little."

"Yes, she is special, that's for sure."

I feel bad that I always appear to be moaning and try to drag myself out of my depression and say firmly, "Anyway, that's all in the past. Who knows, next year could be the making of Polly Proud-lock. Maybe my stars are aligning because I'm not on my own anymore because I have you, your family and Susie, so I am richer than I ever thought possible."

He nods and squeezes my hand. "I'll look after you."

"No, Miles, I'm a big girl now and I don't need looking after. It will all work out, I'm a great believer in fate and the fact that I'm a superhero's sidekick assures me of my success in life."

Suddenly, I step away from my depression and see the future calling. I am leaving this all behind and heading into the new year a different person. It's not so bad, I can do anything because I've found love and with Miles by my side, I am invincible.

We decide to head to a nearby pub after ice skating, to grab something to eat, and once we are settled in front of the inglenook fireplace, I stretch out in contentment. "This feels sooo good."

Miles nods. "I could get used to this. I don't know, life here is certainly less frantic than London. I used to think it was what I wanted, but now I'm not so sure."

My ears prick up and I say with interest, "What do you mean?"

He shrugs. "It's just that I'm not looking forward to going back there, leaving you behind. I like the fact we can meet after work and enjoy the simple things. Maybe I'll relocate here and we can get a flat together if Susie does move in with Scott."

I stare at him in astonishment as hope blooms in my heart. "Really, do you really mean that?"

"Possibly, let's just see how things pan out in the next few months, I think we should consider it an option at least."

"Or I could move to London with you and get a job in a shop or something. That could work."

His eyes twinkle in the light of the fire and I don't think he has ever looked more desirable than at this moment as he says softly, "If I'm with you, Polly, it will always work."

Something snaps inside me and changes everything. I no longer feel depressed, I feel euphoric because he's right, with a man like Miles beside me I can conquer anything. Whatever happens will be what's meant to, and if I never stuff a cracker again, it will be because fate always intended it to be that way. Now I just feel excited and hopeful of a bright future and it's all because I stepped out of my comfort zone and helped a friend in need. If anything depresses me it's the thought I might never have met Miles at all but then again, I think we were always destined to meet one way or another.

CHAPTER 34

*T*oday is my last day at Sparkle Crackers and the office party. We are allowed to wear our Christmas jumpers and a Santa's hat and armed with my secret Santa gift of a tub of Quality Street, lovingly wrapped by Suze, I head into work carrying my food contribution of a packet of sausage rolls and a few family packs of crisps.

I feel upbeat and yet a little sad that one chapter is closing before I know what the next one will bring. But just like the most interesting book, the close of one chapter leads to the next and a happily ever after in the end. I hope that's the sort of book I'm living in because at the moment it feels more like a thriller where the heroine stands to lose everything.

My friends are waiting with excited smiles at the thought of having a week off work and yet there's sadness as we contemplate this being the last time we stand as a team, stuffing novelty items into crackers. I will be gone and Gail will be power dressing on the mezzanine level. That still hurts, but I can't dwell on it now because we have an exciting day ahead.

The music is full of hope and cheer as we sing along to

favourite tracks and swap stories of what our perfect Christmas looks like. Cindy is spending it in Luton with her family and then meeting up with Darren on Boxing day at his parent's home. Marion is going to her eldest son's where she will enjoy a family Christmas with her grandchildren and her other son and his family. I am spending it with Miles and his family and Gail is heading home and then meeting up with Richie on the 27th to go sale shopping.

It must be close to 12.30 when Richie stops by and says to Gail, "Leave that sweetheart, you can help me set up the Christmas party in the canteen."

She smiles with excitement. "Thanks, honey, I'd love that." He nods to the rest of us and then says with interest. "So, what does it feel like being here for the last time, Polly, do you have anything else lined up?"

He smirks, which annoys me, so I smile brightly and look enthusiastic. "Yes, I'm moving to London with my boyfriend. I'm getting a job there and starting a new exciting chapter in my life. I'll think of you all here though, I hope it works out."

He looks a little put out, which makes me laugh to myself. I'm glad I won't have to see him after today, and if anything, I feel more sympathy for Gail than envy at being saddled with a creep like that. Thank God he dumped me and I never thought I'd say that. Miles is so much better, and if nothing else goes right in my life ever again, I would still count my blessings that I found him.

1.30 ARRIVES and we all head to the staff canteen for the annual office party. We have all swapped Christmas cards, addresses and Christmas wishes and now is the final hurdle to jump before heading home for a well deserved break. The room has been transformed from the rather shabby industrial one to Santa's grotto, with paper chains hanging from the ceiling, merging with red and green balloons. A Christmas tree stands proudly in the corner, around which are the many secret Santa's gifts donated by the workers. A buffet table is struggling to hold the various donations of food that everyone was instructed to bring and the paper cups of wine and soft drinks stand waiting for the hordes to descend.

Loud music is playing to create a party atmosphere and as is normal, all the tables are set with Sparkle Crackers and bowls of nuts and crisps.

Grabbing one with Marion and Cindy, we are soon joined by Darren and a few of the guys from the warehouse. The noise is all around us as we chat amongst ourselves, while sipping substandard wine and eating more carbs and sugar than a body should be subjected to.

Marion laughs out loud when she sees one of the drivers stumbling in a little worse for wear, dressed in a Santa's costume and shouts, "Ho Ho Ho, have you been naughty or nice this year?"

There are many screams of 'naughty' as he showers chocolate coins around the room like confetti.

I make sure to take many photos and videos to look back on because despite how much we all moan about this place, we love it really. We are like a family, a band of people united by our job, and the thought that this room will be empty next year, or holding a different type of Christmas party, is a sad one indeed.

One by one, we head up to greet Santa as he hands out the secret Santa parcels and there is much hilarity as people unwrap cheap gifts, many of them distasteful and near the mark. Marion laughs as she holds up an apron with a pair of boobs and a thong printed on it and squeals, "My Derek will think he's won the lottery when he sees me in this."

Cindy squeals as she drops a pair of fluffy pink handcuffs on the table and her boyfriend winks at her and grins. I unwrap a Toblerone which I am more than happy about and after a lot more wine and some quite frankly dubious dancing, we are brought into line when the music is silenced and someone claps their hands.

"Listen up everyone, Mr Sullivan would like to say a few words."

The party atmosphere disappears completely as our much loved owner stands before us looking a little sheepish. He clears his throat and says loudly, "I just wanted to wish you all a happy Christmas and thank you for working so hard this year. I can't pretend it was a good one business wise and I hate the fact that for many of you this will be your final one with us."

He clears his throat and then we all look surprised as he turns to the door and waves at someone and we see two men walk into the room dressed in suits looking a little ominous. Marion hisses, "Who are they?"

"I don't know?" I shrug and feel my heart beating madly as I sense change on the horizon.

Richie is looking surprised which shows even he doesn't know what's coming, and then Mr Sullivan clears his throat again and smiles warmly. "As it happens, now is the perfect time to make an announcement. You know that things have been difficult for a few years and we have had to make some drastic changes to how we operate. Business isn't as good as it once was, but it could be again. I have been exploring all avenues to reach a solution to our problems and keep Sparkle Crackers going, and not just existing but thriving. Miss Constable did a good job and I was sad to see her go but I'm a great believer that everything happens for a reason as I'm sure you will soon agree."

My heart lurches as he pulls a bundle of familiar stationery from his pocket and smiles.

"It appears that I have a secret admirer."

The laughter ripples around the room like a Mexican wave, and I feel my face burning as he reads out some of my ideas. Then he looks at the crowd and says loudly, "I'm sure you'll agree, this was a bold move by someone who certainly knows their crackers. The thing is, it came too late for Sparkle Crackers as you know it."

My heart sinks. Then he calls out, "Gail, can you come up here please."

A gentle murmur follows her as Gail walks on wobbly legs over to stand beside him and he beams at her. "It was brought to my attention that the mystery letter writer is none other than our amazing novelty worker Gail Donaldson."

What the... My mouth drops open in shock as Mr Sullivan grins. "Gail's ideas are amazing and she deserves this chance to see them through. At the last management meeting, I brought up the subject of the letters and Richie Banks informed me that it was Gail who sent them. Apparently, she confided in him and he helped to deliver the letters to me. It was ingenious and certainly nothing like I have ever seen in all my years of business. Well, as I said before, it was a little late but then something happened yesterday that secured Sparkle Cracker's future.

I still can't process the speed at which the full horror of my situation is delivering blows on me. Richie Banks double crossed me. He gave my job to someone else and sacked me. I can't believe it.

$\mathcal{I}$'m in shock as Mr Sullivan carries on. "I would like to introduce you to Mr Jones and Mr Mortimer from J S Holdings. They are keen to buy the company and move it on to the next level. Along with Gail and her ideas, I am sure your futures are guaranteed, not to mention that Sparkle Crackers will live on.

"Excuse me."

From out of nowhere a voice rings out loudly and somebody steps up in the crowd. My heart beats frantically as I realise it's *me*.

Somehow, I have found some backbone and decided not to take the blows anymore but to fight back and Mr Sullivan smiles as he says, "Is there something you want to say?"

"Yes, actually, just one thing."

Richie is looking at me furiously and to her credit, Gail just looks surprised, making me think she hasn't a clue about the identity of the real letter writer.

"Mr Sullivan, please can you do me a favour and honour the contents of that letter?"

He looks confused and I warm to my subject as every pair of eyes in the room are fixed on me with astonishment.

"Sir, I'm afraid to say that the person who wrote those letters is not standing beside you. Gail never wrote them despite what Richie Banks tells you."

Richie quickly whispers something in Mr Sullivan's ear and I see the disappointment on his face as he says softly, "I'm sorry my dear, but this isn't helping. I know you have lost your job, but making a scene isn't the answer."

I glare at Richie with the tightest fury and say angrily, "If you don't believe me, then ask Gail what the letter asks you to do at the staff party?"

Gail's face burns and she looks at Richie for support, who is heading my way with a furious expression, no doubt intent on manhandling me from the room. Mr Sullivan looks at Gail and says kindly, "Ok, Gail, what did you ask me to do?"

I feel bad for Gail because she has been caught up in something she didn't really understand and she shakes her head and says loudly, "I didn't write those letters."

There's a gasp from the crowd as all eyes are riveted on the scene, her words stopping Richie in his tracks. Mr Sullivan looks confused. "Then who did?"

Resisting the urge to roll my eyes, I say firmly, "Mr Sullivan, the letter states that if you like the ideas in the letter, you will ask the person to step forward at the company Christmas party. *I am* that person and those are my letters. Mr Banks has made it his business to ruin my chances and put his girlfriend in my place out of revenge for me turning him down when he assaulted me in his office last week."

A huge gasp of collective horror echoes around the room and Marion shouts, "Disgusting, but I'm not surprised."

Gail's eyes are wide as she says in a shaky voice, "Is that true, Richie, did you assault Polly?"

"Don't be ridiculous, everyone knows she's bitter because

I dumped her. She's just stirring up trouble and trying to make a scene out of anger at being made redundant."

He turns to me and says tightly, "I'm sorry it didn't work out between us, Polly, but you really must stop spreading these lies."

Marion shouts, "Bloody liar."

The noise erupts in the room as everyone adds their own voices until Gail shouts, "Stop."

We all look at her in surprise as she stands there shaking with rage. She fixes Richie with a look that could kill and spits, "Polly's right, I believe every word she said. You told me the contents of those letters and made out it was your idea, Richie. You told me to pretend they were mine and between us we would work together to get a promotion. You made me think it was for our future because you loved me. I know you don't. When you saw Polly with her new boyfriend, you were jealous. I knew it but didn't want to face it. Then when you called Polly to your office on the pretence of a verbal warning, I saw her face when she came back. She was shaken and upset, and the fact your lip blew up like a balloon told me everything I needed to know."

"Shut up Gail, you don't know what you're talking about."

Suddenly, Rachel from ribbons stands up and says loudly, "Richie assaulted me too."

The room falls silent as all eyes turn to her and she says with a quivering voice. "He made me meet him in his office and told me if I was nice to him, I would keep my job. Needless to say, today is my last day, I'm better than that."

The hurt on Gail's face will live with me forever as her world crashes from under her. Richie is bright red and murmurs of 'disgusting' and 'pervert' rumble around the room, and Mr Sullivan fixes him with a look that could wither a plant in seconds. "Mr Banks, I expect to see you in my office, now."

As Richie storms out he leaves a silent room as we stare after him in shock. Then all eyes turn to Mr Sullivan, who is obviously apoplectic with rage. He looks at me and says softly, "Please sit down, Miss…"

"Proudlock, sir. Polly Proudlock."

He smiles. "Thank you, Miss Proudlock. Please accept my apologies for everything you have gone through. Come and see me at the end of the day, we have much to discuss."

He turns to Gail and says somewhat kindly, "Miss Donaldson, needless to say your promotion has been revoked. However, your old position remains, if you want it that is."

Gail nods meekly and says gratefully, "I do, I'm sorry, sir."

She hurries back to her chair and I am heartened to see the person next to her put their arm around her and whisper words of comfort.

Mr Sullivan looks around the room and shakes his head. "Well, that was a Christmas surprise I never saw coming. Anyway, I just wanted to reassure you all of the future and wish you a very Happy Christmas. Mr Mortimer will be taking charge next year and I will stick around for six months in a handover period. I just want to take this opportunity to thank you all for all your hard work over the years and wish you every success in your future, hopefully with Sparkle Crackers at the centre of it."

As he smiles and leaves the room with the two men in tow, Marion and Cindy stare at me with astonishment. I shrink a little under their gaze and say nervously, "That went well, I think."

Marion leans across and hugs me fiercely and whispers, "Don't forget us when you rise to management level. We'll be cheering you on from the base line."

Cindy has tears in her eyes as she smiles through them. "Good luck, Polly, that was a very brave thing you did and you are an inspiration to us all. I really hope you won't be leaving and stay."

I feel myself relax for the first time since I was handed my redundancy, and a huge wave of relief calms me inside. It worked. Miracles do happen, and sometimes it's up to us to steer them in the right direction when they blow off course.

CHAPTER 36

*B*y the time I make my way out of the canteen, I feel more nervous than I ever have before. I wonder what will happen as I make my way up the hallowed steps to the mezzanine level. Before I get there though, a small voice stops me in my tracks. "Polly."

Turning, I see Gail looking hesitant nearby and she looks so miserable I reach out and pull her in for a big hug, saying gently, "You didn't know, it's ok."

For a moment she clings to me and I whisper, "I'm so sorry, Gail."

Pulling back, she smiles briefly and yet her misery is hard to ignore. "No, it's me who should be sorry. I trusted Richie and he told me lots of lies saying that you were pestering him to take you back, its why I was so cold towards you. Then he told me about cracker suggestions and made out they were his big plan. I swear I didn't know about the letters, the first I heard of them was earlier. I was so embarrassed and of course I had to speak up. I may not be perfect, but I hope I'm a good friend when it counts."

The tears are brimming in her beautiful blue eyes and I

feel a surge of pity for the girl who I once called my nemesis. "It's fine, Gail, I'm sorry you were in that situation in the first place. What will you do now?"

"Oh, I don't know." She shrugs. "Well, I think we can safely say that Richie and I are finished. I heard he's been fired and escorted from the building by Harry. It will be a little awkward retrieving my stuff from his flat, but I know it's the right thing to do. I may look for another job, though. I'll hang on until I find something, but it holds a few painful memories now and I really think I'd like to start again somewhere new."

I feel sorry to hear that and say sadly, "That's a shame. Mind you, I'm not sure of my own future yet, I'm just on my way to find out what that is."

The nerves return and she smiles brightly. "You'll be fine, you deserve this chance. After all, you did something bold and hopefully it will pay off. You're an inspiration Polly, I'd like to learn from your example and one day maybe I'll change my life for the better."

"Well, make sure you keep in touch and I'll look forward to seeing how it all turns out."

She nods and then heads off, a dejected figure that has lost a lot today, although she may not think so now, she is so much better off without Richie Banks in her life. Thinking of the man himself, I hope he got what he deserved. He used his position of power at Sparkle Crackers to assault women, and they went along with it in fear of losing their job. Now my rose coloured spectacles are no longer in place, I can see that was exactly the basis of our own relationship. He never loved me, he used me, and I was the fool who let him.

My heart thumps as I head upstairs, and I can't wait to see Miles later and tell him what happened today. I hope he will be proud of me for standing up for myself. I should have done it much sooner and not worried about what other people thought of me.

It feels strange being in the corridors of power. It's not a place I usually frequent, and my heart is racing as I prepare to face a man I have only ever watched from my position below his feet. Mr Sullivan has always maintained distance from the shop floor, using people like Richie Banks to oversee the workers and report back. Maybe that's why his business stopped running with the competition, perhaps it's why he failed. Surely, it's good business practice to use all your resources and the opinions of his staff should have mattered, after all, we are customers too.

I approach his office and see Mrs Barrett typing away, surrounded by strings of brightly coloured Christmas cards and piles of tinned biscuits and chocolates on the shelf behind her. Many of these find their way downstairs to the shop floor which I should be grateful for, but then I notice the multitude of bottles resembling a small off-licence and smile inside as I contemplate their home at the end of the day. Certainly not downstairs, I'm sure they have a more salubrious ending in sight.

Miss Barrett looks up and smiles. "Ah, Polly, Mr Sullivan is waiting for you."

"Am I late?" I look at her nervously and she shakes her head. "Not at all, please don't worry, it'll be fine, relax."

I nod, but my nerves have tangled my confidence in a death grip because I have never felt so nervous in my life. Thinking of the words I wrote - on pink paper for goodness' sake, what must he think of me? Perhaps he really thought I was a secret admirer, I wouldn't blame him, I mean, who writes a letter to their boss with a business opportunity on pink paper? An idiot, that's who and I feel like the biggest one alive as I knock on his door and hear a low voice growl, "Enter."

Mr Sullivan's office has definitely seen better days. Like the rest of the factory, the paint is peeling and the furniture outdated and unfit for purpose. The filing cabinets are bent out of shape and no longer close properly. The carpet on the floor is threadbare and slightly faded and the ceiling has a brown stain running the length of it where I expect some water got in and was never freshly painted. There is a slightly musty smell in here, and the blinds at the window are old fashioned and broken at the bottom. Piles of paperwork sit on every surface and Mr Sullivan's desk is crowded with files, stained tea mugs and more pens than a stationery shop. The man himself is sitting on a wheelie chair looking at me with interest and I stand a little straighter as he says enthusiastically, "Ah, Miss Proudlock, it's good of you to come."

"Thank you, sir."

I can't think what else to say and he nods towards the chair in front of his desk. "Please take a seat, Polly, am I allowed to call you that?"

"Of course, sir."

As I settle in place, he suddenly looks serious. "Firstly, may I offer you my most sincere apologies for what you have gone through. Mr Banks was operating as a wild card in this organisation and it should have been detected sooner. Needless to say, he has been fired and is now the subject of a police enquiry. The safety of my staff is my number one concern and harassing them is an unforgiveable offence."

I can't feel sorry for Richie because he deserves all the trouble coming his way and just feel relieved that I won't have to see him again.

Then Mr Sullivan leans back and laughs softly. "I must say Polly, in all my years of business I have never been captivated by a letter as much as I was yours. I couldn't believe what I was reading and after I recovered from the shock, I was impressed."

"I'm sorry, sir."

"What for?"

"For being bold enough to criticise your business, it was a little harsh."

"Nonsense, I'm a big boy and only a fool would ignore well meaning criticism. I should have taken my head out of the sand years ago and actually asked my staff for their input. If I've learned anything it's that, so that leads me to your future."

My nerves are now out of control as I hitch my breath, wondering what's coming. I think I have all my fingers and toes crossed for luck because my future hinges on the words he's about to say.

"I would like to offer you the job you applied for, Polly. As a development manager working alongside Mr Mortimer, the new owner of Sparkle Crackers. You will report to him and present your ideas and will occupy an office nearby with Miss Barrett at your disposal. How does that sound?"

I did it, I actually did it and my plan paid off. I have achieved greatness with the brush of a pen and bold ambition. My smile is the biggest one to ever grace my face and I say with delight, "Thank you so much, Mr Sullivan. I'm ecstatic. I really want to make a difference and make this work."

"I know you do, Polly, we need people like you in business, people with a passion for what they do. I lost sight of that myself for a while and just got bogged down with spreadsheets and balance sheets. The business needs fresh ideas and motivated people to keep it alive. Well done Polly Proudlock, you now have the opportunity to shine."

He looks down at his desk and then hands me a sheet of paper. "Now for the boring bit. Please fill in your details and sign this contract. It replaces your old one and you will see the wages reflect your new responsibilities. Once you've agreed and signed the contents, you are free to go home and enjoy Christmas. I must just say one thing Polly, you have taught me a valuable lesson here."

I look up and he appears thoughtful.

"There's no point in putting all your resources into selling something that your customer no longer wants. All the promotions and discounts in the world count for nothing if the product is wrong. You were right that people won't consider the cost if they want something badly enough, and I was blind to that. Now you've opened my eyes, I see it's obvious. All around me, other industries have developed and adapted to provide what people want. They are surviving because of it. Never lose sight of that Polly, because that is the blood of the business that keeps the heart beating. I wish you well my dear and look forward to seeing your ideas on the shelves in those stores that gave up on us when they saw what I couldn't."

He smiles warmly, "Now off you go and enjoy the break. I'll look forward to seeing you bright and early on the 2nd January, Miss Proudlock, don't let me down."

"I won't, Mr Sullivan, thank you for believing in me, I will do everything in my power to make this work, you can rely on me."

For a moment, we share a look of understanding. The old giving way to the new. Past, present and future at a crossroads with an exciting path to follow instead of the dead end it was facing a few days ago. If Christmas does bring miracles, this is a bright one because now the people downstairs and Sparkle Crackers can head into the New Year with a lifeline.

CHAPTER 37

"I knew you'd do it."

Miles is sitting with his arms wrapped tightly around me while we watch a film on the Christmas channel.

"It could have backfired though if Richie had his way, can you actually believe that happened?"

"We'd have sorted it out, he wouldn't have got away with it. In fact, now he's facing a criminal charge as a result."

I snuggle in, happy to be in the only place I really want to be, Miles's arms.

He kisses the top of my head lightly. "I have some news of my own."

Spinning around, I look at him with surprise and he smiles. "I couldn't tell you before, but after today it's no secret. I'll be working from Harpenden for the first part of next year, possibly longer."

"You are?" I can't believe it and he nods. "You know that project I've been working on?"

"The one that's kept you working until the early hours."

"Yes, well, it was handling the acquisition of Sparkle Crackers, actually."

My face must be a picture because he looks a little nervous. "You're not angry, are you?"

I'm not sure how I feel because it all seems a little odd. Did he use me for information to find out all the inner secrets of a business he was pursuing for someone else? I feel a little used and he must notice my concern because he holds my face in his hands and says firmly, "Look at me Polly."

I have no other choice and he says, "I was working on this before I met you. It was just the most amazing coincidence, and anything you told me never made it past my lips. I couldn't tell you because it was top secret and may never have happened. My clients were undecided and believe it or not, it was your letters that swayed their opinion."

"My letters." I feel weak with anxiety as I imagine the pink paper finding its way into executive hands, and he laughs. "Mr Sullivan showed them your ideas and they were impressed. They came to me not knowing I was involved with you on a personal level and told me that they liked the ideas and saw a potential future for a new type of cracker. They were going to look into the costings involved and inject the capital needed to get the project off the ground. It gave them something to work with and they were keen to seize the opportunity, so I managed to negotiate a deal that kept both parties happy. Mr Sullivan gets a huge payout for his company and a seat on the board with a percentage of future profits. The consortium, headed up by Mr Mortimer, gets a company for much less than it could be worth the same time next year and the chance to be the leaders in their field. I suppose what swayed it was the type of product on offer. Christmas is always coming every year without fail. People will always want to celebrate that and traditions count for a lot. Cards, crackers and gifts are as much a part of Christmas as the reason for it in the first place. It's the traditions that keep it magical and my clients recognised that and saw a future for a product that just needed a makeover."

"But…"

He leans down and captures my words with a long passionate kiss and nothing else matters. He's right, Christmas is a magical time and this year the magic was directed at me.

We pull apart quickly when the front door slams and Susie heads into the room, looking weary under the weight of several bags of last minute shopping. She drops them with a groan. "Remind me to do all my shopping in November next year. The crowds are insane out there."

Jumping up a little guiltily, I try to hide my red face by saying quickly, "Let me grab you a coffee, I was just about to make one."

Miles throws me a wicked grin as Susie rolls her eyes, "Sure you were."

She flops down in the chair opposite and I leave them to chat while I head off to the kitchen.

As I make the drinks, I feel a little stupid, after all, Miles is my boyfriend and Susie is not my mum and well, our relationship is probably at the point where we should be taking things further. I am keen to move it on but I do quite like the way things are now. What if I ruin things by taking it to another level and then the magic dies? I couldn't bear that to happen, so I hold back. If Miles got bored with me, I don't think I'd recover from this one. Nothing is straight forward it seems and not being an expert at relationships, this one is a difficult one to call.

As it turns out, Susie is now in for the evening and Miles has to leave to carry on working on the Sparkle Crackers acquisition, so it leaves me free to ponder my problem for another day. Why, when you have it all, is there always something more?

∽

CHRISTMAS EVE ARRIVES with a different kind of excitement this year because for the first time since I was a child, I am looking forward to Christmas. Today is going to be a busy one because Susie is leaving for home this morning and I am helping her pack. It's my job to make sure she has everything she needs and by the time we've finished, her little Fiat is crammed so full I'm worried it's a fire hazard. She can just about see out of the windows and it strikes me she has a bit of a shopping problem. If I remember correctly, it's only her parents and brother for Christmas, yet she appears to have more gifts in her car than Santa's sleigh, and as she slams the car door shut, she groans.

"I may have gone a little overboard again this year. Maybe I should have got that set of golf clubs delivered to their house instead of insisting it was delivered here and wrapping it up to resemble a giant cracker. It seemed like a good idea at the time."

Susie is always overly generous at Christmas and I picture the number of parcels beautifully wrapped under our tree upstairs that she left for me and it brings a lump to my throat. She always over indulges me at every occasion that requires a gift, and I know it's to compensate me for the lack of any from my family. In fact, hers are the only actual gifts I can look forward to unwrapping because mum always gives me a voucher and dad transfers £20 on Boxing day as a last-minute thought. Thinking of Susie's own loving family just highlights the fact mine are so bad and so I hug her tightly and say emotionally, "Have a safe journey and enjoy Christmas. Try not to think of anything other than having the best time with your family."

For a moment we stand in the street hugging as if we are never going to see each other again, and despite the fact it's beginning to snow, I am reluctant to let her go. Susie Mahoney has become like a sister to me and along with Miles, is the most important person in my life.

After a while, she pulls back and shivers, but I see the emotion in her eyes that she always tries to disguise. I know she feels bad for me and wishes I had a family like hers. She is always inviting me to spend time with them, I suppose hoping they will adopt me as one of their own and for the most part they do. I love her crazy family and would love nothing more than to spend Christmas with them, they always insist, but I always head to my mothers in the vain hope that one day she will actually want me there.

However, this year I have bucked the trend and am spending it with Miles and his family and I can't wait. Pauline and Elvis have been so welcoming, and I am keen to spend time with them. Miles is coming here this afternoon and we are going last-minute shopping, followed by a cosy meal by the river, and after a few drinks we are spending the rest of the evening preparing for tomorrow. It all feels so exciting and as if we have always been a couple and I'm hopeful for the future.

Susie smiles and says tearfully, "Have a Happy Christmas, Polly, you deserve it."

"You too. Try not to think about Scott at least until Boxing day."

She nods and I hate seeing the uncertainty in her eyes as she sighs. "I think I know what I'm going to do, but I'll talk it through with mum. She's quite good at these sorts of things and will set me on the right path."

Thinking of Susie's broad-minded mother, I feel the usual pang of envy when I dwell on the relationship they share. I suppose not everyone knows how to be that perfect mother. Mine certainly didn't read the manual and appeared to skip the actual growing up part. However, Susie's mum passed the exam at the end with flying colours and I know that her advice will be good advice, so I wave Susie off in the knowledge that she will return with a clear head and a decision on her future that will be the right one.

As her car disappears into the distance, I stand for a moment as the snow falls a little heavier. The air is crisp and pure and I see the hustle and bustle all around me of anticipation and excitement for the most magical day of the year and for once I feel it too. As I turn to head back to the flat, it's with an alien spring in my step. Somehow, I made it. I got everything I wanted and it didn't need gift wrapping. Gifts don't matter because what I have is worth so much more. I have a bright future ahead of me and it's thanks to stepping outside my comfort zone and trying something new, that got me here.

CHAPTER 38

*C*hristmas Day dawns and I wake up with a smile on my face and it's all because of the man sleeping peacefully beside me.

Miles stayed the night last night and it all happened so naturally I don't know what I was worried about. This is it; we are now officially in love and a couple that will face the world together. For a moment, I relive the most special evening of my life when after a busy day spent cleaning, wrapping and shopping, we enjoyed a special meal for two by the water's edge and ended up here for hot chocolate and a nightcap. I lit candles and we snugged down, side by side on the settee and watched 'The Night Before Christmas.' It felt so right and this time when our kisses deepened and the passion grew, I pushed any fears away and smashed through the final hurdle and it was every bit as amazing as I always knew it would be. Yes, Polly and Miles are now officially a couple and I couldn't wish for a better present than that.

Leaving him to sleep, I make my way into the small kitchen and flick the kettle on. It feels a little chilly, so I pull my dressing gown tighter and stupidly smile at the coffee jar.

This year feels so different. Usually I wake up in my mum's house and then have to endure a marathon session watching her new family unwrap their brightly wrapped presents from Santa with a painted smile on my face. All I felt was pain as she whispered that she hoped she had remembered everything on their list because she would hate it if they were disappointed. The only thing I ever hoped for was a little bit of thought and warmth from a mother who stopped trying years ago. However, this year it doesn't matter because I have Miles and am now part of something so much better.

The phone interrupts my thoughts and I'm surprised to see my dad's name on the display. This is unusual, so I answer with a nervous, "Hi dad, Happy Christmas."

"Hi babe, same, what are you up to today?"

I can't remember the last time we spoke and feel a little surprised to hear his voice at all. Usually it's Boxing day before he remembers me but it feels nice to hear his voice, so I say happily, "I'm spending it with my boyfriend and his family this year."

"That's good, babe, I'm happy to hear that, it's about time you put yourself first for once and made your mum do some of the work for a change."

His words surprise me because he never really seemed bothered that I was enduring Christmas hell at my mother's house and then he says with unusual emotion, "I'm sorry, Polly."

"For what?" I feel a little alarmed at the pain in his voice and wonder if he has something terrible to tell me. The anxiety grips me hard as I say fearfully, "Is everything ok dad?"

"Yes, babe, everything's fine. In fact, I have some news, but first I want to apologise for being an absent father all these years."

"It wasn't your fault…"

He interrupts. "Of course, it was my fault, Polly. I was a rubbish father to you and well, I just want to apologise for that and maybe try and make amends."

"Oh."

I'm not sure what to say because this is unexpected. Maybe he had a bump to the head after a few drinks last night and has woken up a changed man. It's like a film I once saw, I'm sure it must be something like that.

He carries on. "You must be wondering if I've been on the sherry already, but I'm stone cold sober, I promise. It's just, well, you remember I got married a few months ago?"

"Yes." My heart pounds as I sense change coming and wonder if it's something that will burst the cosy bubble I woke up inside.

He laughs softly and I relax a little. "Well, Melanie is finally coming home and we are looking for a house to buy. I'm retiring from the Navy and we decided to settle in Harpenden to be near you."

This is news and I'm not sure what to say, but there is something growing inside me that is making me hope for yet another miracle this Christmas and I almost can't wait to hear his next words.

"You'll like Melanie, babe, she's a great woman."

"But I thought she was from Thailand, by the sounds of it she's…"

"English." He chuckles and carries on, "Melanie worked for the foreign office in Thailand. She's a secretary and we met at a welcome party when the ship docked in port there. Well, as you know, we kind of clicked and kept in touch, then when I got leave I flew out to stay with her. To cut a long story short, we married and always intended to set up home here in the UK, after all, it's where we're from. Well, Melanie is keen to meet you and hates the fact we're not as close as we should be. I've told her everything and she's a good listener. I feel so guilty at how I left you to fend for yourself over the years and was an absent father. Well, I want that to change and I want to start that process now, if you want to meet us that is."

He sounds so anxious I feel bad for him, despite how lonely his absence made me all these years, so I say warmly, "What did you have in mind?"

"Meet us tomorrow, I've booked a table at Luton Hoo. I can increase it to four if you want to bring your boyfriend. I need to check he's suitable, after all."

I can't help the huge smile that breaks out across my face as I hear the emotion in his voice. Then the tears form as I realise, I've got my father back. He may have left it a little late, but he's here and willing to try to be the father I wanted all these years. My voice breaks making me realise how much this means to me and I say through my tears, "I would love that, dad. I can't wait to meet Melanie."

His voice shakes as he whispers, "I can't wait to see you again babe, I've missed you."

"Me too, dad."

I can almost picture him awkwardly holding the phone, trying to deal with a situation he will feel uncomfortable with. He has never been an emotional man, and this has come as a huge surprise of the nicest kind. I have my dad back and that is the greatest gift of all.

We chat for a little before we arrange to meet at Luton Hoo at 2 pm the next day and as I cut the call, Miles appears in the doorway looking sleepy but wearing a huge smile on his face.

"Happy Christmas, Polly Galore, our first one together but one of many I hope."

He heads across and wraps me in his arms, and every-thing is right with my world. I have him, my father, and now Melanie. Miles's family have welcomed me as one of their own and for all her faults, I have my mother too. Susie is still the most important person in my life because she is the kindest, most loyal friend I could have ever wished for and I have a new job, a glittering career and a bright future to look forward to. My life begins today and for the first time, I don't feel alone anymore.

Miles pulls back and grins with excitement.

"Come on, I've got you something."

"What is it?"

"You'll see."

He winks as I follow him to the little Christmas tree that stands by the window, the fairy lights twinkling, their reflection in the window making them brighter as they sparkle against the snow on the ledge outside. We even have a white Christmas, another first. Usually it's raining, or just dull, but this year it's like a Hallmark movie outside and inside is no different as we grasp our hot steaming mugs of coffee and kneel at the foot of the tree, wrapped warmly in our dressing gowns. Miles hands me a small package, beautifully wrapped, and his eyes sparkle.

"This is for you."

I take a moment to appreciate the designer touches that can only have been placed there by one person. "Pauline?"

He laughs. "Sorry, I wanted it to be special and she insisted she wrap it for you."

"It's lovely, in fact this could be the present itself because it's too gorgeous to destroy."

The little white box decorated with red ribbon and a twig of berries looks so delightful I'm almost tempted to take a picture for Instagram. In fact, I decide to do just that and make Miles wait until I grab my phone and record the moment for posterity.

Then I carefully hold the small box and wonder what could be inside. My fingers shake as I unwrap a beautiful silver bracelet and then admire the charm of a silver cracker hanging proudly from it."

Miles says anxiously, "Do you like it, I wasn't sure if you would wear something like this."

"I love it Miles."

My voice is choked with emotion because this is the perfect gift.

He says softly, "I wanted something to build on. I intend on buying you a charm every year for the rest of our lives. Something with meaning that's special to us."

He pulls my face to his and whispers, "I'm so glad I found you, Polly. I just want to say that I know it's only been a few weeks, but I have fallen so madly in love with you, I would do anything to make you happy. I would give up my world for you and I want to make you *my* world. I'm looking forward to the future with you beside me and if that future is here in Slip End, in this flat for the whole of it, then I am happy as long as it's with you."

My heart bursts as we share a kiss that cements our future. As the delicate silver cracker spins on the bracelet and reflects the light, I share the most special moment with the man I love. We pull apart and I say softly, "I love you too Miles, but promise me one thing."

"Anything."

"Next time we go anywhere in fancy dress, you let me choose."

"Of course."

"And another thing."

"Name it."

"We don't spend our lives in a flat in Slip End. We work hard and maybe one day can afford a pretty little house on a nice street in Harpenden."

"Consider it done."

Reaching behind me, I pull out another gift and say shyly, "This is for you."

I feel anxious as I hand him a box that Susie wrapped with her flair and expertise, and he smiles with excitement.

"I wonder what this is?"

"Open it and see."

I'm a little worried that it's nowhere near as thoughtful as the one he gave me, but it's too late now and I wait anxiously for him to open the box and look inside. Along with a bar of his favourite chocolate is an envelope and he looks intrigued. I wonder what he will make of it and as he removes it from the box, he grins. "Is this another one of your letters telling me how I can be a better boyfriend? I'm sorry if I've let things get stale already."

He winks as I nudge him hard and just roll my eyes, as he takes out the piece of paper and brochure that's hidden inside.

He starts to read. "Escape to Happy Ever After with me for a lovely long weekend in May where all your happy endings are guaranteed."

He starts to laugh and I say crossly, "What's so funny?"

"My happy endings are guaranteed. Did you really write this?"

"Of course I didn't, it's what came with the confirmation. Ok, I know it has a double meaning these days but think of it in the spirit of the occasion."

He looks down at the card and smiles, then leans in and pulls me close, dropping a sweet kiss on my lips and saying, "Thank you, it's perfect. If I'm getting any happy endings, I want them to be with you."

"Idiot."

I can't stop the small giggle that escapes as he studies the card.

"Kirrin Cottage, isn't that where the Famous Five lived?"

"I'm impressed. You know your Enid Blyton."

"What self-respecting British child doesn't? I never knew it was an actual place though."

"I know, mad isn't it? I saw it on the Internet when I was surfing for ideas and thought it sounded really cute. It's in Dorset and apparently run by two mad people who think they're Aunt Fanny and Uncle Quentin. I thought it would be interesting to check out."

"That is mad, it looks sweet though."

"It does, you should check out the reviews, nearly all five stars, even though the owners are as nutty as a packet of chocolate covered peanuts. It's what people love about it, so I thought what better place to send my own crazy Batman for a holiday."

"Do you think they would appreciate us turning up in our costumes?"

"I told you, I'm never being Robin again. I'm choosing next time."

We share a grin, and I think this is possibly the happiest I have ever felt on Christmas morning outside of when I was five. Miles makes everything fun and exciting and now we have lunch with his parents to look forward to and I can't wait.

CHAPTER 39

*E*lvis and Pauline greet us on their impressive doorstep dressed as Santa and Mrs Claus and Miles groans. "Oh God, when will they retire those bloody costumes?"

Before we even set one foot through the door, Pauline and Elvis start singing.

♫ "WE WISH *you a merry Christmas, we wish you a merry Christmas, we wish you a merry Christmas and a happy New Year.*" ♫

THEN THEY SHOOT streamers in the air before pulling us in for a hug.

Miles shakes his head and I laugh as the two crazy people bundle us inside and Pauline shouts, "Elvis, take their coats and bags and put them under the tree. Not the coats though, I wouldn't put it past you."

Without stopping for air, she grabs our hands and says

happily, "Jessica's here already although sadly alone again and Freddie and Annabella are five minutes away. Quickly come in and add your name to the sweepstake your father's running as to how many times Annabella tells Freddie off. I'm guessing twenty, Jess says fifteen and dad says five."

We stumble into the room where Jessica sits with a mulled wine and holding a pen poised over a piece of paper, she says quickly, "Come on, I need your guesses before they get here. The winner gets a bottle of dad's finest champagne."

"Bloody hell, Pauline, I thought you said it was a box of matchmakers."

Jessica and Pauline dissolve into giggles and Miles grins. "Same old trick, dad falls for it every time."

He laughs. "Dad has a stash of champagne he's been saving for a special occasion. There never is one so it just keeps on gathering dust and growing every time he adds another bottle to it."

"Chance would be a fine thing for a special occasion. I'm waiting for a wedding, or baby shower to pop those corks with abandon. Anyway, gathering dust are, you serious?" Pauline looks hurt and Miles puts his arm around her and gives her a hug. "Metaphorically speaking of course mum, there's never any dust in this place."

"Meta what? You make these words up to confuse me half the time so I don't say anything. What's he talking about Polly, is that even a word?"

I'm spared from answering when we hear Elvis shout, "Ready for round three, Pauline, they're here."

Pauline rushes to the door and while we hear another rendition of, 'We Wish You a Merry Christmas,' we quickly add our guesses to the list.

I am interested to see Annabella again and hope she has settled down a bit, for Freddie's sake. Maybe she was nervous before , after all, it must be true love for her to spend Christmas with her boyfriend's family rather than her own.

As she heads into the room, she looks irritated and just nods, "Hi guys, I never thought we'd make it here alive. Freddie's driving was seriously off today, I think he must still be hungover from the drinks he insisted on going to with his friends last night. I told him he should have come to church with me and my family, it is a tradition, after all. Well, give him no sympathy if his head hurts because it's all self-inflicted."

I watch Jessica write something down and smile to myself, number one ticked off, how many more to go?

Freddie comes in beaming broadly and looks more relaxed than Annabella as he hugs his sister and then pulls me into an equally affectionate hug. "Good to see you, girls, did Santa bring you anything worth having this year?"

Jessica nods. "A day off, that's the greatest gift I could have."

Pauline shakes her head. "I keep on telling her she should slow down, it's not healthy working all the time."

"I disagree, Mrs Carlton, when you are young you need to work hard to play hard later. You don't get anywhere in life by lounging around watching tv and sleeping your life away. Take me for instance. I am usually up at 6am and straight on the hot water to cleanse my system. Then I do an hour's yoga and meditation before breakfast and I'm still at my office desk by 8am. Routine is a necessity in every young person's life and I don't waste a minute of mine. You see, that is why I will succeed and it won't be because I'm lucky, it will be because I have engineered my success and planned it."

She sniffs as she takes a glass of mulled wine that Pauline hands her and says haughtily, "Is this homemade, Pauline because I am against the shop blended products on offer. Full of sugar and substitutes. My mother always makes up a bouquet garni in advance and pops it into the superior red wine that we keep for the occasion, along with a cinnamon stick and clove studded orange."

She sniffs her drink and looks mildly disgusted and Pauline says tightly, "Oh no, Annabella, this is no ordinary mulled wine, it's..."

We all shout, "M&S mulled wine."

Then we dissolve into fits of laughter as Annabella looks around in surprise. Before she can say anything, Pauline says loudly, "Anyway, grab your glasses and head into the living room. There are a few nibbles in there and dad wants to show you the video he took when we went to the Christmas market in Vienna. Jess can help me sort out the starters because she's seen it already."

Miles whispers, "Prepare yourself, Polly, Mum is a Christmas Ninja and I doubt you'll ever be the same again after today.

Looking over at his mum, I see her looking a little stressed and biting her bottom lip. She is apparently consulting a big clipboard decorated in tinsel and running her finger down the pages. Then she looks at her watch and shouts to Jess. "I need a pan of boiling water for the Christmas pudding. It needs to start steaming now, or all those months of marinating will be in vain."

She catches me watching and says efficiently, "Christmas starts early in this house, Polly. Christmas pudding day is somewhere in October where I have a day when I stir until my arm falls off. Be careful though, there are a few pieces of silver in it, one for everyone so we all have good luck this year."

She looks at her sons and pulls a face. "God knows we need some this year."

Then she shouts, "When you've done that, Jess, I need to get started on the plum sauce. Make sure your hands are washed and ready, we don't have long."

Annabella looks bored already as Freddie takes her hand and leads her quickly out of the room and Miles slings his arm around my shoulders. "It's probably best if we leave them to it. Once mum gets started on the dinner, only a fool would stick around."

Pauline shouts, "What do you mean, get started. I started this meal weeks ago, not to mention getting up at the crack of dawn just to stuff a turkey in the oven. It's not easy being a domesticated goddess you know."

Pauline shakes her head. "Whatever, anyway, this meal won't make itself, so shoo everyone and let the maestro create."

As we head into the living room, Miles groans. "Sorry, I forgot to tell you about dad and his videos."

"It's fine, I'm quite interested really, I've never been to a Christmas market."

"Then consider yourself invited to one next year." He drops a light kiss on my forehead and smiles softly. "I want to give you everything, Polly, within reason, of course."

He winks and I smile happily. "I've already got everything I want right here."

"For goodness sake, what's keeping you, hurry up, the video's loading."

We quickly rush into the living room and I absolutely love the huge sparkling tree set in the bay window, guarding piles of presents glittering below. The fire is crackling in the huge inglenook fireplace and candles burn on every surface. There's an intoxicating scent of cinnamon and orange, courtesy of the diffusers on the tables and little bowls of nuts and crisps mingle with plates of canapes and other enticing appetisers.

I have never spent a Christmas like this and would watch Elvis's whole video collection, happily sitting beside Miles with my feet tucked up on their comfortable couch. This is perfect, they are perfect and I wouldn't want it any other way.

CHAPTER 40

*B*y the time we are called into Christmas dinner, I think I'm in love with Vienna. It looked so magical and just like a fairy tale and Miles whispered that it would be us taking a coach ride around the city next year, which made me feel warm inside. The fact that my mother hasn't even called ceases to matter.

Miles and his family make me feel like one of them, and even the constant sniping of Annabella does little to dampen my spirits. Poor Freddie, though. First, she was too cold and then too hot. She made him swap places with her several times and told him off for sitting untidily. When he spoke, she told him to be quiet and not interrupt the viewing and he couldn't say, or do, anything right for the entire time. Miles and Elvis kept on sharing looks that made my heart ache for Freddie because it's obvious they don't approve of his choice and who can blame them.

I'm not sure what he sees in her, but maybe she is different when they're alone.

She keeps on looking at her watch and after a while, I

hear her whisper, "How much longer, did you tell them we have to leave by three?"

Freddie looks uncomfortable and Elvis says loudly, "What's the matter, son?"

"Um, sorry, but we have to leave at 3 o'clock, Annabella's parents have booked a table at a nearby hotel in Guildford and we can't be late."

Pauline chooses that moment to come in and announce that dinner is ready and looks at Freddie with a mixture of hurt and disbelief. "What are you talking about, you always spend the evening here too. When was this arranged?"

Annabella rolls her eyes. "I can't believe you didn't tell them. I told you to phone ahead and now they think we're rude."

Turning to Pauline, she says bluntly, "My parents have arranged Christmas supper at an exclusive hotel near to Guildford. We can't be late, so may just have to skip lunch here and just leave our gifts and go. I'm sorry, but Frederick should have told you."

Freddie looks miserable and says apologetically, "I'm sorry mum but I didn't know until this morning. It was arranged as a last-minute solution for us spending the day with both sets of parents. I hope you understand."

I almost daren't look at Pauline because I know she'll be devastated and to her credit, she just smiles bravely. "Of course, I understand. Well, maybe you can have a starter at least and then we'll bundle up your presents and you can head off."

Freddie looks wretched and Elvis just looks angry but Annabella looks at her nails and says dismissively, "Honestly Freddie, apologise to your parents, that was so rude."

Surprisingly, it's not Pauline, or Elvis who steps in but Jessica who has obviously had enough and says angrily,

"Excuse me, Annabella, but why don't you just give it a rest for once? If anyone is rude around here it's you, not Freddie."

Annabella opens her mouth and Jessica shouts, "Don't even think about saying anything. I have sat and watched you moan about everything since I met you. You look down your nose at us and treat Freddie as if he's an idiot. You criticise, disapprove and are quite frankly, rude and ignorant. Well, why don't you just grab your things and go if that's what you want because you're ruining Christmas for the rest of us."

"Jessica!"

Elvis looks angry as Jessica storms from the room, leaving the rest of us speechless behind her. Freddie looks embarrassed and doesn't appear to know where to look first and Miles steps in and says gently, "Come on, let's all go and eat something. One course is better than none. Jessica doesn't mean it; she's just upset for mum."

Annabella's face is like thunder, but she thinks better of saying anything else and follows Freddie into the dining room. Miles looks upset and I catch a look on Pauline's face that tears at my heart. Elvis whispers something in her ear and she nods and smiles before shaking herself and saying brightly, "Come on then, it's Christmas day after all."

Some of the magic has gone and been replaced by a false atmosphere, and my heart goes out to a family that only wanted everyone to be happy and welcome. I feel so angry at Annabella and hope that Freddie wakes up and sees sense before things get serious.

Pauline turns her attention to organising everyone and I notice beautifully written place settings edged in gold glitter glue, standing proudly before beautiful china and crystal glasses. She starts ordering everyone into their place and I love the fact there is a beautifully decorated box on everyone's plate with their name on it. I settle down next to Elvis and Miles and Pauline says to her husband, "Elvis, make sure everyone has a drink."

We suddenly hear a rendition of Jingle Bell Rock coming from the kitchen and Jessica says, "I think the vegetables are ready to go on, mum."

Pauline appears to strike an item off her checklist and nods. "On time, that's good. I'll turn them on while you grab the prawn cocktails. Make sure they are sprinkled with a little paprika and a squeeze of lemon juice before you serve them. I'll fetch the granary bread."

"Is there anything I can do to help, Pauline?"

I feel bad because it appears Pauline is buckling under the weight of a feast and she smiles gratefully. "Just enjoy yourself, darlin', that's all I want from you."

Annabella turns to Freddie and says loudly, "I didn't know prawn cocktail was still a thing, how nostalgic."

Pauline just glares at her before heading off and soon the sound of pans crashing makes its way from the kitchen and Miles whispers, "I'm guessing mum's taking out her frustrations on the cookware again, at least dad's safe for a while."

"I feel sorry for her." I lower my voice to a whisper. "She's gone to so much trouble and Annabella is looking down her nose at just about everything, she's so rude."

Then we hear a piercing alarm ring out from the kitchen and Pauline yells, "Elvis, I told you to disconnect that bloody heat detector, you know how sensitive it is."

Elvis jumps up and raises his eyes. "Sensitive my foot, that bloody woman would burn this house down given half a chance."

As we sit in an awkward silence waiting for them to join us, I wonder about the relationship between Annabella and Freddie. They seem well suited on the outside but are poles apart in personalities. He's good-natured and laid back, and she's so uptight she may snap like one of my crackers at any moment. Maybe it's a case of opposites attract, or their sex life makes up for everything. Either way, I still can't see them working. I'm not sure why, but my thoughts turn to my best friend who is in a similar predicament. She would be so much better than Annabella for Freddie. In fact, the more I think of it, the more I get excited about it. Could I stage an intervention and somehow get them together? Vowing to talk to Miles about it later, I look with interest as Pauline heads into the room, looking a little red faced as she carries a tray of glasses, stuffed full of delicious looking prawn cocktails, in glasses decorated with a sugar crust and a twist of lemon.

"Are you ok mum?"

Freddie laughs as Pauline starts dishing out the starter. "I just got a little close to the oven when I opened it. The steam gave me an instant facial."

We laugh as she starts to giggle and Annabella shakes her head. "It's important to look after one's skin. I myself have a strict beauty regime and never cut corners. Some people ignore the most valuable part of their body and age terribly."

She looks across at me and smirks, "What products do you use, Pollyanna?"

"Um, it's Polly actually, Annabella, I do hate being called anything other than my name."

Pauline bursts out laughing and Annabella looks irritated as I throw her own pet hate right back at her. I'm done with being polite and I suppose she's rubbed me up a little too much because I instantly feel bad and say to Pauline, "This all looks amazing, thank you so much, you've worked really hard."

Miles raises his glass along with the rest of us and says brightly, "To mum and Christmas. It wouldn't be the same without her."

As we all toast the woman who has gone to so much

trouble to make it special, I notice a tear in her eye as she shares a look with Elvis who smiles his approval and mouths, "Happy Christmas, babe."

It leaves me with a warm feeling inside, seeing how happy they still are after years of marriage. In fact, they are all happy, which makes Freddie's decision even stranger. I can't for the life of me understand what he was thinking when he hooked up with the ice queen opposite.

We all sit down to our starters and the food tastes as good as any posh restaurant that Annabella's parents have booked, better in fact. It doesn't take us long to polish off a course that probably took longer to prepare than to eat, and as I set my cutlery down the beautiful crackers immediately demand my attention and I say with admiration. "Pauline, these crackers have turned out so well. I love the artistic touches; they look so special."

Annabella lifts hers and looks at it closely and then says dismissively, "Good effort, Pauline. My mother always insists on ordering hers from Harrods every year. You can be assured of the quality, not like those cheap ones that the masses enjoy."

By now I think we are all queueing up to tear Annabella off a strip but before we can, Freddie stands up and says angrily, "Enough, Annabella, you've gone too far, we're leaving."

Annabella almost looks ecstatic about that and nods to Pauline and Elvis as she stands.

"Thank you for your hospitality, Mr and Mrs Carlton. Please accept my apologies for Freddie's outburst, I'm not sure what came over him."

Freddie just looks at her with disgust and I think I hold my breath as he says wearily, "I'm sorry everyone, I'll drop Annabella home and if it's ok, I'll head back later tonight. I'll probably be around three hours by the time I've negotiated the M25 and the A3."

"What do you mean, drop me off? We have plans, you're not leaving me to face my parents alone, are you?"

Annabella is furious, it's obvious from her flashing eyes and tight lips and Freddie says firmly, "We'll talk about this in the car. We've ruined enough of their Christmas by being here in the first place. Get your coat, Annabella, we're leaving."

Nobody says a thing. In fact, nobody even looks at anyone else until they leave, banging the door shut behind them.

Then Elvis looks at Pauline and says with relief, "It's a Christmas miracle. I hope you kept the receipts for her presents."

Jessica grins. "If not, I'll have them, I know what they are."

Pauline leans back and shakes her head. "Thank God he opened his eyes. I don't think I could have made it through the meal without stabbing her with the carving knife. My goodness, what on earth did Freddie see in her?"

Jessica looks thoughtful. "I'm guessing it was a case of anyone would do. If I'm not mistaken, he would have paid someone to come here with him just to keep you all happy."

"What do you mean, paid someone? Why would he do that?" Pauline looks astonished and I can feel my face burning as Miles looks at me and winks.

Elvis laughs softly, "Not a bad idea really, I mean, after last year he had to do something."

He looks at Miles with a worried expression. "He probably wanted to show us he's moved on since that wretched business with 'she who must not be named.' Anna, what's her name was probably the best he could come up with in the time he was given."

"But why, Elvis we're his family, why would anyone want to make us think they were happy when they're not?"

"Because we love you."

Miles speaks and I think I hold my breath as he turns to me and takes my hand in his. "To be honest, I had the same idea."

"What?" Pauline looks shocked and I feel like a deer caught in headlights.

"Then I met Polly, and it was no longer an option. You see, like Freddie, I wanted things to get back to normal. For us to be a family again, and Kate tore us apart when she played one brother off against the other. Like me, Freddie felt awkward and just wanted things to get back to normal. In bringing a new girlfriend home, it would prove to everyone that he had moved on and it all worked out in the end."

"Do you think he's still upset over, you know, *her*." Jessica looks worried and Pauline shakes her head. "I don't. Just the fact he tried and put himself through hell by dating a creature like Miss Fancy Pants shows me he is keen to move on. One day he'll meet someone and get his happy ever after, until then he'll flounder around like the rest of us did, making mistakes until one of them leads him to the love of his life."

I catch Miles's eye and we share a look. Yes, we know all about that and if I'm sure of anything, it's that miracles do happen and Freddie will get his happy ever after one day and the fact we're about to go off and enjoy ours, gives me hope that his isn't that far away either.

CHAPTER 41

I feel bad for Freddie because he has missed the best Christmas meal that I have ever eaten. Pauline was in a frenzy as she dished up a Christmas dinner that would be the pride of any Michelin starred chef. Somehow, even an ordinary roast dinner is made special as she proudly explains the various dishes on offer alongside a potted history of how she made each one from scratch and even used some vegetables she grows in her garden. Pauline is a domestic goddess and a Christmas Angel all rolled into one.

As expected, her crackers interest me the most and as we pull them, I love the confetti that showers onto the table along with a little gift wrapped in tissue paper that certainly didn't originate from the novelty line at Sparkle Crackers. Mine holds a lovely silver charm for my bracelet in the shape of a candy cane and Pauline says happily, "To add to your collection, Poll, it's to remind you of your first Christmas with us a member of our family."

I'm not sure I can form words as she gives me the kindest gift I have ever received, the gift of a family. Pauline and

Elvis have made me feel so welcome I couldn't have wished for anything more, and as Miles's hand finds mine under the table, we lace our fingers together and I'm so happy I could burst.

The cracker jokes are actually funny enough to raise a small laugh in place of the usual groans and there are no paper hats, just interesting hairbands with different titles on each. I am an angel; Pauline is Mrs Christmas and Miles an elf. Jessica is a fairy and Elvis Santa. I wonder what Annabella's would have been, but am too afraid to ask for fear of dampening everyone's spirits.

The pudding is brought out to loud claps and cheers which turn to laughter when Elvis pours half a bottle of brandy on it and sets fire to it with a blow torch. Pauline's shrieks have permanently damaged my ear drums as she moans about her lovingly prepared pudding being cremated before it had even lived.

Dessert wine, cheese, mince pies and Christmas cake, all make an appearance and it's with considerable relief that we all slump in front of the fire, unable to lift a finger for at least an hour.

Pauline and Jessica finally agree to receiving some help and I love working with them, clearing away the chaos of Christmas while listening to carols on the radio while the men watch a programme on cars.

Freddie makes it back as he thought, three hours later and goes straight to his mum and wraps her in a bear hug, saying gruffly, "I'm sorry mum."

She shakes her head and smiles. "It's fine, babe, but I'm worried about you."

"Don't be, I'm ok. Just not that good at picking women it would seem."

Jessica shakes her head. "You can say that again, leave it with me, I'll fix you up with one of my friends."

"What, Sally slut or Fiona the f…"

"Mum, I told you about them in confidence."

Freddie's eyes light up. "I like the sound of them both, do you think…"

"No, Freddie, you need a nice girl, not an easy one. Leave it with me, I'll look through my approved list on Dream Beginnings."

"Your what?"

Freddie looks horrified and Elvis interrupts, "You don't know the half of it, son. Mum's got a list drawn up of suitable partners for everyone, even her if I pop my clogs."

"Not Miles, Polly, I shifted his list to Freddies when I met you."

Pauline looks at me guiltily and I laugh. "I'd love to see that list."

Jessica grins. "Actually, it's worth a laugh, if nothing else. Mum's idea of a dream partner for her children is probably different to anyone else's. What's the criteria again mum, oh yes, good prospects, a certain age, good-looking but not enough to make them a player. Interesting hobbies, and she has drawn up a questionnaire any potential dates must fill in before being granted a meeting. It's actually hilarious."

Elvis groans, "The only one who doesn't have a list is me. I'm not allowed to even login to the bloomin' site and yet Pauline has a virtual mood board for men she likes the look of depending on her mood at the time. No equal opportunities in this house, Poll, I'm just the sucker that pays for it all."

Pauline winks at me before moving across to her husband and planting a kiss on his lips. She whispers something to him and I watch his eyes light up and he looks at his watch. "Are you all still here, haven't you got homes to go to?"

Miles shares a look with his siblings who look a little disgusted and I laugh to myself as Pauline and Elvis share a long lingering kiss by the tree before Pauline pulls back and says with excitement, "Come on Freddie, I've kept your dinner warm. While you catch us up, your dad can dish out the presents. It will take him long enough for you to eat your meal without rushing, and then we can all sit down and see what Santa left us."

Jessica flops down beside me and says with excitement, "Prepare yourself, Polly, mum starts shopping in the January sales, you could be here for some time."

∾

WE FINALLY LEAVE AROUND 11 pm, armed with more presents than we came here with and the memory of the perfect Christmas, well at least once Annabella had left. Freddie was newly single and yet didn't seem bothered. In fact, he was much better company without his girlfriend and decided to stay for a few days to spend time with his family. We left to return to the flat because we have a Boxing day treat lined up with my father to look forward to.

For the first time in forever, I feel content, happy and full of hope for the future.

Christmas can be a very lonely time for those with nobody who cares, and I was always grateful that at least I had an invitation to my mum's, despite how painful an experience it was.

Now I have a future to look forward to with the man I love and his amazing family, and that is worth more than anything else that's happened.

As we head home after the happiest day, I look around at the winter scene we pass. The light from the headlights picks up the flurry of snow that is carpeting the road with a little piece of magic, and Miles turns up the heat and the soft sound of Silent Night filters through the speakers. Reaching across he grasps my hand and says sweetly, "Happy Christmas, darling, I just want to tell you that I love you and can't wait to escape to Happy Ever After with my fellow caped crusader."

Raising his hand to my lips, I kiss it softly and say with contentment, "I can't wait."

The End

BEFORE YOU GO

If you've read My Christmas Boyfriend, you will know just where Miles and Polly are heading when they Escape to Happy Ever After.

For those of you who haven't read that one yet, check it out, it still remains my favourite Christmas story.

And guess what, Escape to Happy Ever After is coming sooner than you think. It's the title of my January release and you can catch up with some old friends when two books collide and happy endings are guaranteed.

Order Now

As it's Christmas I have a special gift that you can unwrap today. You will find it hidden on the next few pages – happy hunting!

Thank you for reading My Christmas Romance.

If you liked it, I would love if you could leave me a review, as I must do all my own advertising.

This is the best way to encourage new readers and I appreciate every review I can get. Please also recommend it to your friends as word of mouth is the best form of advertising. It won't take longer than two minutes of your time, as you only need write one sentence if you want to.

Have you checked out my website?

Subscribe to keep updated with any offers or new releases.

When you visit my website, you may be surprised because I don't just write Romantic comedy.

I also write under the pen names M J Hardy & Harper Adams. I send out a monthly newsletter with details of all my releases and any special offers but aside from that you don't hear from me very often.

I do however love to give you something in return for your interest which ranges from free printables to bonus content. If you like social media please follow me on mine where I am a lot more active and will always answer you if you reach out to me.

Why not take a look and see for yourself and read Lily's Lockdown, a little scene I wrote to remember the madness when the world stopped and took a deep breath?

sjcrabb.com

Lily's Lockdown

(Just scroll to the bottom of the page and click the link to read for free.)

If you want to know how Finn and Lily met check out

.

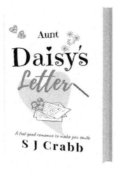

Aunt Daisy's Letter

By the way – that isn't the gift – keep going!

More books by S J Crabb

My Christmas Boyfriend

After what is going down in history as the worst day of her life – so far – Annie Anderson, finds herself on a train heading home for Christmas.

Going against all the laws of travelling on British Rail, she strikes up a conversation with the angry man opposite. After downing his supply of brandy (residing in a convenient hip flask) they soon discover they have something in common.

He needs a girlfriend and she needs a boyfriend – for Christmas anyway.

In a haze of brandy fumes, she agrees to be his date to a family wedding. In return, he will accompany her home and play the role of her boyfriend for Christmas.

With no regard for her safety, armed only with Dutch courage, and her sense of adventure, she follows him into what can only be described, as the craziest Christmas ever.

Be prepared for Christmas overload.

KEEP IN TOUCH

You can also follow me on the Social media below. Just click on them and follow me.

Facebook

Instagram

Twitter

Website

Bookbub

Amazon

CHRISTMAS TRIVIA

What is Christmas without some cracker jokes to make you groan louder than when you are faced with the Brussel sprouts?

Here are some to make you groan.

Why are chocolate buttons rude? Because they are Smarties in the nude.

What do you get if you cross Santa with a duck? A Christmas quacker!

What's big, grey and wears glass slippers? Cinderelephant.

What do you call a donkey with three legs? A wonky.

What did the grape say when someone stood on it? Nothing. It just let out a little wine.

What athlete is warmest in winter? A long jumper.

What do you get if you cross a bell with a skunk? Jingle Smells!

Why do Giraffes have long necks? Because their feet smell.

Why did the turkey cross the road? Because he wasn't chicken

What do Santa's little helpers learn at school? The elfabet.

Who hides in the bakery at Christmas? A mince spy!

What do you call a short-sighted dinosaur? A do-you-think-he-saw-us!

Doctor, doctor I keep thinking I'm a budgie. Don't worry, I've got some tweetment for that.

Lollipop ladies make me cross.

What breed of dog can jump higher than a building? Any type of dog, buildings can't jump.

What do you call a sleeping bull? A bulldozer.

What do you get if you cross a kangaroo with a sheep? A woolly jumper.

Still not the gift though – here it is!!!

The Ultimate Christmas Planner.

Be super-organised this year with a daily 'To Do' list of all things Christmas. Be a Pauline and nail it with a daily task to make sure you have the best Christmas.

Download your free Calendar and feel like a domesticated goddess as you strike every item off your list and arrive at Christmas day feeling certain everything is in order.
For paperback versions please drop me an email at scrabbauthor@gmail.com and I will send you your gift.

My Christmas Planner

The History behind The Christmas Cracker.

Christmas crackers are a traditional Christmas favourite in the UK. They were first made in about 1845-1850 by a London sweet maker called Tom Smith. He had seen the French 'bon bon' sweets (almonds wrapped in pretty paper) on a visit to Paris in 1840. He came back to London and tried selling sweets like that in England and also included a small motto or riddle in with the sweet. But they didn't sell very well.

Legend says that, one night, while he was sitting in front of his log fire, he became very interested by the sparks and cracks coming from the fire. Suddenly, he thought what a fun idea it would be, if his sweets and toys could be opened with a crack when their fancy wrappers were pulled in half.

In 1861 Tom Smith launched his new range of what he called 'Bangs of Expectation'! It's thought that he bought the recipe for the small cracks and bangs in crackers from a fireworks company called Brock's Fireworks.

Crackers were also nicknamed called 'cosaques' and were thought to be named after the 'Cossack' soldiers who had a reputation for riding on their horses and firing guns into the air.

When Tom died, his expanding cracker business was taken over by his three sons, Tom, Walter and Henry. Walter introduced the hats into crackers and he also travelled around the world looking for new ideas for gifts to put in the crackers.

The company built up a big range of 'themed' crackers. There were ones for bachelors and spinsters (single men and women), where the gifts were things like false teeth and wedding rings! There were also crackers for Suffragettes (women who campaigned to get women the vote), war heroes and even Charlie Chaplain! Crackers were also made for special occasions like Coronations. The British Royal Family still has special crackers made for them today!

Very expensive crackers were made such as the 'Millionaire's Crackers' which contained a solid silver box with a piece of gold and silver jewellery inside it!

Cracker manufacturers also made large displays, such as horse drawn carriages and sleighs, for the big shops in London.

The Christmas Crackers that are used today are short cardboard tubes wrapped in colourful paper. There is normally a Cracker next to each plate on the Christmas dinner table. When the crackers are pulled - with a bang! - a colourful party hat, a toy or gift and a festive joke falls out! The party hats look like crowns and it is thought that they symbolise the crowns that might have been worn by the Wise Men.

The world's longest Christmas cracker measured 63.1m (207ft) long and 4m (13ft) in diameter and was made by the parents of children at Ley Hill School and Pre-School, Chesham, Buckinghamshire, UK on 20 December 2001. Now that would be one big bang!

The biggest Christmas cracker pull was done by 1,478 people at an event organised by Honda Japan at Tochigi Proving Ground, Tochigi, Japan, on 18 October 2009. Now that would be a lot of bangs!

Taken from whychristmas.com

ESCAPE TO HAPPY EVER AFTER

Remember to order your Happy Ever After. We could all do with one of them. xxxx

Order Now

Printed in Great Britain
by Amazon